The LITTLE HOUSE Books — A Pioneer Chronicle

"If our country can become great in humility, and can work earnestly to solve its own problems at the same time that it carries its share of world responsibilities, it will be through vision of our children, their integrity and idealism, gained in homes like the home in the 'Little House' books."—*The Horn Book*

"Any boy or girl who has access to all the books in the series will be the richer for their first-hand record of pioneer life in the opening West and for their warm-hearted human values."—*The New Yorker*

"One of the phenomenal achievements in modern literature for children, a genuine chronicle for American life and of family life at their equal best. Through these books Laura Ingalls of the 1870's and '80's has stepped from pages of the past into the flesh and blood reality of a chosen friend."—*The Horn Book*

"Among the most popular books written for boys and girls are . . . the 'Little House' series which relates the experiences of the author's own family . . . in establishing various homes in the days when the western lands were opened up to settlers."—*Library Journal*

"It is a matter of great satisfaction and a cause for gratitude that . . . we can turn to such a group of stories as those (of) Mrs. Wilder . . . (They) ring true in every particular. Their authentic background, sensitive characterization, their fine integrity and spirit of sturdy independence, make them an invaluable addition to our list of genuine American stories."—*The New York Times*

FARMER BOY

Books by Laura Ingalls Wilder

LITTLE HOUSE IN THE BIG WOODS

LITTLE HOUSE ON THE PRAIRIE

FARMER BOY

ON THE BANKS OF PLUM CREEK

BY THE SHORES OF SILVER LAKE

THE LONG WINTER

LITTLE TOWN ON THE PRAIRIE

THESE HAPPY GOLDEN YEARS

Newly illustrated, uniform edition printed 1953

Farmer Boy

by LAURA INGALLS WILDER

ILLUSTRATED BY GARTH WILLIAMS

A HARPER TROPHY BOOK

Harper & Row, Publishers
New York, Evanston, San Francisco, London

FARMER BOY

Text copyright 1933 by Laura Ingalls Wilder
Copyright renewed 1961 by Roger L. MacBride
Pictures copyright 1953 by Garth Williams.

First published in 1933. 26th printing, 1953.
Revised edition, illustrated by Garth Williams,
published in 1953. 13th printing, 1970.

First Harper Trophy Book printing, 1971.

ISBN 0-06-440003-4

CONTENTS

Chapter 1. SCHOOL DAYS 1

Chapter 2. WINTER EVENING 13

Chapter 3. WINTER NIGHT 30

Chapter 4. SURPRISE 39

Chapter 5. BIRTHDAY 49

Chapter 6. FILLING THE ICE-
HOUSE 65

Chapter 7. SATURDAY NIGHT 75

Chapter 8. SUNDAY 84

Chapter 9. BREAKING THE CALVES 95

Chapter 10. THE TURN OF THE
YEAR 109

Chapter 11. SPRINGTIME 120

Chapter 12. TIN-PEDDLER 133

CONTENTS

Chapter 13. THE STRANGE DOG 141

Chapter 14. SHEEP-SHEARING 154

Chapter 15. COLD SNAP 163

Chapter 16. INDEPENDENCE DAY 173

Chapter 17. SUMMER-TIME 190

Chapter 18. KEEPING HOUSE 203

Chapter 19. EARLY HARVEST 228

Chapter 20. LATE HARVEST 240

Chapter 21. COUNTY FAIR 252

Chapter 22. FALL OF THE YEAR 275

Chapter 23. COBBLER 285

Chapter 24. THE LITTLE BOBSLED 299

Chapter 25. THRESHING 305

Chapter 26. CHRISTMAS 312

Chapter 27. WOOD-HAULING 329

Chapter 28. MR. THOMPSON'S POCKETBOOK 344

Chapter 29. FARMER BOY 362

FARMER BOY

Chapter 1

School Days

IT WAS January in northern New York State, sixty-seven years ago. Snow lay deep everywhere. It loaded the bare limbs of oak and maples and beeches, it bent the green boughs of cedars and spruces down into the drifts. Billows of snow covered the fields and the stone fences.

Down a long road through the woods a little boy trudged to school, with his big brother Royal and his two sisters, Eliza Jane and Alice. Royal was thirteen years old, Eliza Jane was twelve, and Alice was ten. Almanzo was the youngest of all, and this was his first going-to-school, because he was not quite nine years old.

He had to walk fast to keep up with the others, and he had to carry the dinner-pail.

"Royal ought to carry it," he said. "He's bigger than I be."

Royal strode ahead, big and manly in boots, and Eliza Jane said:

"No, 'Manzo. It's your turn to carry it now, because you're the littlest."

Eliza Jane was bossy. She always knew what was best to do, and she made Almanzo and Alice do it.

Almanzo hurried behind Royal, and Alice hurried behind Eliza Jane, in the deep paths made by bobsled runners. On each side the soft snow was piled high. The road went down a long slope, then it crossed a little bridge and went on for a mile through the frozen woods to the schoolhouse.

The cold nipped Almanzo's eyelids and numbed his nose, but inside his good woolen clothes he was warm. They were all made from the wool of

2

his father's sheep. His underwear was creamy white, but mother had dyed the wool for his outside clothes.

Butternut hulls had dyed the thread for his coat and his long trousers. Then mother had woven it, and she had soaked and shrunk the cloth into heavy, thick fullcloth. Not wind nor cold nor even a drenching rain could go through the good fullcloth that mother made.

For Almanzo's waist she had dyed fine wool as red as a cherry, and she had woven a soft, thin cloth. It was light and warm and beautifully red.

Almanzo's long brown pants buttoned to his red waist with a row of bright brass buttons, all around his middle. The waist's collar buttoned snugly up to his chin, and so did his long coat of brown fullcloth. Mother had made his cap of the same brown fullcloth, with cozy ear-flaps that tied under his chin. And his red mittens were on a string that went up the sleeves of his coat and across the back of his neck. That was so he couldn't lose them.

He wore one pair of socks pulled snug over the

3

legs of his underdrawers, and another pair outside the legs of his long brown pants, and he wore moccasins. They were exactly like the moccasins that Indians wore.

Girls tied heavy veils over their faces when they went out in winter. But Almanzo was a boy, and his face was out in the frosty air. His cheeks were red as apples and his nose was redder than a cherry, and after he had walked a mile and a half he was glad to see the schoolhouse.

It stood lonely in the frozen woods, at the foot of Hardscrabble Hill. Smoke was rising from the chimney, and the teacher had shoveled a path through the snowdrifts to the door. Five big boys were scuffling in the deep snow by the path.

Almanzo was frightened when he saw them. Royal pretended not to be afraid, but he was. They were the big boys from Hardscrabble Settlement, and everybody was afraid of them.

They smashed little boys' sleds, for fun. They'd catch a little boy and swing him by his legs, then let him go headfirst into the deep snow. Sometimes they made two little boys fight each

4

other, though the little boys didn't want to fight and begged to be let off.

These big boys were sixteen or seventeen years old and they came to school only in the middle of the winter term. They came to thrash the teacher and break up the school. They boasted that no teacher could finish the winter term in that school, and no teacher ever had.

This year the teacher was a slim, pale young man. His name was Mr. Corse. He was gentle and patient, and never whipped little boys because they forgot how to spell a word. Almanzo felt sick inside when he thought how the big boys would beat Mr. Corse. Mr. Corse wasn't big enough to fight them.

There was a hush in the schoolhouse and you could hear the noise the big boys were making outside. The other pupils stood whispering together by the big stove in the middle of the room. Mr. Corse sat at his desk. One thin cheek rested on his slim hand and he was reading a book. He looked up and said pleasantly,

"Good morning."

Royal and Eliza Jane and Alice answered him politely, but Almanzo did not say anything. He stood by the desk, looking at Mr. Corse. Mr. Corse smiled at him and said,

"Do you know I'm going home with you tonight?" Almanzo was too troubled to answer. "Yes," Mr. Corse said. "It's your father's turn."

Every family in the district boarded the teacher for two weeks. He went from farm to farm till he had stayed two weeks at each one. Then he closed school for that term.

When he said this, Mr. Corse rapped on his desk with his ruler; it was time for school to begin. All the boys and girls went to their seats. The girls sat on the left side of the room and the boys sat on the right side, with the big stove and wood-box in the middle between them. The big ones sat in the back seats, the middle-sized ones in the middle seats, and the little ones in the front seats. All the seats were the same size. The big boys could hardly get their knees under their desks, and the little boys couldn't rest their feet on the floor.

6

Almanzo and Miles Lewis were the primer class, so they sat on the very front seat and they had no desk. They had to hold up their primers in their hands.

Then Mr. Corse went to the window and tapped on it. The big boys clattered into the

entry, jeering and loudly laughing. They burst the door open with a big noise and swaggered in. Big Bill Ritchie was their leader. He was almost as big as Almanzo's father; his fists were as big as Almanzo's father's fists. He stamped the snow from his feet and noisily tramped to a back seat. The four other boys made all the noise they could, too.

Mr. Corse did not say anything.

No whispering was permitted in school, and no fidgeting. Everyone must be perfectly still and keep his eyes fixed on his lesson. Almanzo and Miles held up their primers and tried not to swing their legs. Their legs grew so tired that they ached, dangling from the edge of the seat. Sometimes one leg would kick suddenly, before Almanzo could stop it. Then he tried to pretend that nothing had happened, but he could feel Mr. Corse looking at him.

In the back seats the big boys whispered and scuffled and slammed their books. Mr. Corse said sternly:

"A little less disturbance, please."

For a minute they were quiet, then they began again. They wanted Mr. Corse to try to punish them. When he did, all five of them would jump on him.

At last the primer class was called, and Almanzo could slide off the seat and walk with Miles to the teacher's desk. Mr. Corse took Almanzo's primer and gave them words to spell.

When Royal had been in the primer class, he had often come home at night with his hand stiff and swollen. The teacher had beaten the palm with a ruler because Royal did not know his lesson. Then Father said,

"If the teacher has to thrash you again, Royal, I'll give you a thrashing you'll remember."

But Mr. Corse never beat a little boy's hand with his ruler. When Almanzo could not spell a word, Mr. Corse said,

"Stay in at recess and learn it."

At recess the girls were let out first. They put on their hoods and cloaks and quietly went outdoors. After fifteen minutes, Mr. Corse rapped on the window and they came in, hung

9

their wraps in the entry, and took their books again. Then the boys could go out for fifteen minutes.

They rushed out shouting into the cold. The first out began snowballing the others. All that had sleds scrambled up Hardscrabble Hill; they flung themselves, stomach-down, on the sleds and swooped down the long, steep slope. They upset into the snow; they ran and wrestled and threw snowballs and washed one another's faces with snow, and all the time they yelled as loud as they could.

When Almanzo had to stay in his seat at recess, he was ashamed because he was kept in with the girls.

At noontime everyone was allowed to move about the schoolroom and talk quietly. Eliza Jane opened the dinner-pail on her desk. It held bread-and-butter and sausage, doughnuts and apples, and four delicious apple-turnovers, their plump crusts filled with melting slices of apple and spicy brown juice.

After Almanzo had eaten every crumb of his

turnover and licked his fingers, he took a drink of water from the pail with a dipper in it, on a bench in the corner. Then he put on his cap and coat and mittens and went out to play.

The sun was shining almost overhead. All the snow was a dazzle of sparkles, and the wood-haulers were coming down Hardscrabble Hill. High on the bobsleds piled with logs, the men cracked their whips and shouted to their horses, and the horses shook jingles from their string of bells.

All the boys ran shouting to fasten their sleds to the bobsleds' runners, and boys who had not brought their sleds climbed up and rode on the loads of wood.

They went merrily past the schoolhouse and down the road. Snowballs were flying thick. Up on the loads the boys wrestled, pushing each other off into the deep drifts. Almanzo and Miles rode shouting on Miles' sled.

It did not seem a minute since they left the schoolhouse. But it took much longer to go back. First they walked, then they trotted, then they ran, panting. They were afraid they'd be late. Then they knew they were late. Mr. Corse would whip them all.

The schoolhouse stood silent. They did not want to go in, but they had to. They stole in quietly. Mr. Corse sat at his desk and all the girls were in their places, pretending to study. On the boys' side of the room, every seat was empty.

Almanzo crept to his seat in the dreadful silence. He held up his primer and tried not to breathe so loud. Mr. Corse did not say anything.

Bill Ritchie and the other big boys didn't care. They made all the noise they could, going to their seats. Mr. Corse waited until they were quiet. Then he said:

"I will overlook your tardiness this one time. But do not let it happen again."

Everybody knew the big boys would be tardy again. Mr. Corse could not punish them because they could thrash him, and that was what they meant to do.

Chapter 2

Winter Evening

THE air was still as ice and the twigs were snapping in the cold. A gray light came from the snow, but shadows were gathering in the woods. It was dusk when Almanzo trudged up the last long slope to the farmhouse.

He hurried behind Royal, who hurried behind Mr. Corse. Alice walked fast behind Eliza Jane in the other sled-track. They kept their mouths covered from the cold and did not say anything.

The roof of the tall red-painted house was

rounded with snow, and from all the eaves hung a fringe of great icicles. The front of the house was dark, but a sled-track went to the big barns and a path had been shoveled to the side door, and candlelight shone in the kitchen windows.

Almanzo did not go into the house. He gave the dinner-pail to Alice, and he went to the barns with Royal.

There were three long, enormous barns, around three sides of the square barnyard. All together, they were the finest barns in all that country.

Almanzo went first into the Horse-Barn. It faced the house, and it was one hundred feet long. The horses' row of box-stalls was in the middle; at one end was the calves' shed, and beyond it the snug henhouse; at the other end was the Buggy-House. It was so large that two buggies and the sleigh could be driven into it, with plenty of room to unhitch the horses. The horses went from it into their stalls, without going out again into the cold.

The Big Barn began at the west end of the

Horse-Barn, and made the west side of the barn-yard. In the Big Barn's middle was the Big-Barn Floor. Great doors opened onto it from the meadows, to let loaded hay-wagons in. On one side was the great hay-bay, fifty feet long and twenty feet wide, crammed full of hay to the peak of the roof far overhead.

Beyond the Big-Barn Floor were fourteen stalls for the cows and oxen. Beyond them was the machine-shed, and beyond it was the tool-shed. There you turned the corner into the South Barn.

In it was the feed-room, then the hog-pens, then the calf-pens, then the South-Barn Floor. That was the threshing-floor. It was even larger than the Big-Barn Floor, and the fanning-mill stood there.

Beyond the South-Barn Floor was a shed for the young cattle, and beyond it was the sheep-fold. That was all of the South Barn.

A tight board fence twelve feet high stood along the east side of the barnyard. The three huge barns and the fence walled in the snug

15

yard. Winds howled and snow beat against them, but could not get in. No matter how stormy the winter, there was hardly ever more than two feet of snow in the sheltered barnyard.

When Almanzo went into these great barns, he always went through the Horse-Barn's little door. He loved horses. There they stood in their roomy box-stalls, clean and sleek and gleaming brown, with long black manes and tails. The wise, sedate work-horses placidly munched hay. The three-year-olds put their noses together across the bars, they seemed to whisper together. Then softly their nostrils whoosed along one another's necks; one pretended to bite, and they squealed and whirled and kicked in play. The old horses turned their heads and looked like grandmothers at the young ones. But the colts ran about excited, on their gangling legs, and stared and wondered.

They all knew Almanzo. Their ears pricked up and their eyes shone softly when they saw him. The three-year-olds came eagerly and thrust their heads out to nuzzle at him. Their

16

noses, prickled with a few stiff hairs, were soft as velvet, and on their foreheads the short, fine hair was silky smooth. Their necks arched proudly, firm and round, and the black manes fell over them like a heavy fringe. You could run your hand along those firm, curved necks, in the warmth under the mane.

But Almanzo hardly dared to do it. He was not allowed to touch the beautiful three-year-olds. He could not go into their stalls, not even to clean them. He was only eight years old, and Father would not let him handle the young horses or the colts. Father didn't trust him yet, because colts and young, unbroken horses are very easily spoiled.

A boy who didn't know any better might scare a young horse, or tease it, or even strike it, and that would ruin it. It would learn to bite and kick and hate people, and then it would never be a good horse.

Almanzo did know better; he wouldn't ever scare or hurt one of those beautiful colts. He would always be quiet, and gentle, and patient;

17

he wouldn't startle a colt, or shout at it, not even if it stepped on his foot. But Father wouldn't believe this.

So Almanzo could only look longingly at the eager three-year-olds. He just touched their velvety noses, and then he went quickly away from them, and put on his barn frock over his good school-clothes.

Father had already watered all the stock, and he was beginning to give them their grain. Royal and Almanzo took pitchforks and went from stall to stall, cleaning out the soiled hay underfoot, and spreading fresh hay from the mangers to make clean beds for the cows and the oxen and the calves and the sheep.

They did not have to make beds for the hogs, because hogs make their own beds and keep them clean.

In the South Barn, Almanzo's own two little calves were in one stall. They came crowding each other at the bars when they saw him. Both calves were red, and one had a white spot on his forehead. Almanzo had named him Star. The

18

other was a bright red all over, and Almanzo called him Bright.

Star and Bright were young calves, not yet a year old. Their little horns had only begun to grow hard in the soft hair by their ears. Almanzo scratched around the little horns, because calves like that. They pushed their moist, blunt noses between the bars, and licked with their rough tongues.

Almanzo took two carrots from the cows' feed-box, and snapped little pieces off them, and fed the pieces one by one to Star and Bright.

Then he took up his pitchfork again and climbed into the haymows overhead. It was dark there; only a little light came from the pierced tin sides of the lantern hung in the alleyway below. Royal and Almanzo were not allowed to take a lantern into the haymows, for fear of fire. But in a moment they could see in the dusk.

They worked fast, pitching hay into the mangers below. Almanzo could hear the crunching of all the animals eating. The haymows were warm with the warmth of all the stock below, and the hay smelled dusty-sweet. There was a smell, too, of the horses and cows, and a woolly smell of sheep. And before the boys finished filling the mangers there was the good smell of warm milk foaming into Father's milk-pail.

Almanzo took his own little milking-stool, and a pail, and sat down in Blossom's stall to milk her. His hands were not yet strong enough to milk a hard milker, but he could milk Blossom and Bossy. They were good old cows who gave down their milk easily, and hardly ever switched a stinging tail into his eyes, or upset the pail with a hind foot.

He sat with the pail between his feet, and milked steadily. Left, right! swish, swish! the streams of milk slanted into the pail, while the cows licked up their grain and crunched their carrots.

The barn cats curved their bodies against the corners of the stall, loudly purring. They were sleek and fat from eating mice. Every barn cat had large ears and a long tail, sure signs of a good mouser. Day and night they patrolled the barns, keeping mice and rats from the feed-bins, and at milking-time they lapped up pans of warm milk.

When Almanzo had finished milking, he filled the pans for the cats. His father went into Blossom's stall with his own pail and stool, and sat down to strip the last, richest drops of milk from Blossom's udder. But Almanzo had got it all. Then father went into Bossy's stall. He came out at once, and said,

"You're a good milker, son."

Almanzo just turned around and kicked at the straw on the floor. He was too pleased to say any thing. Now he could milk cows by himself; Father needn't strip them after him. Pretty soon he would be milking the hardest milkers.

Almanzo's father had pleasant blue eyes that twinkled. He was a big man, with a long, soft brown beard and soft brown hair. His frock of brown wool hung to the tops of his tall boots. The two fronts of it were crossed on his broad chest and belted snug around his waist, then the skirt of it hung down over his trousers of good brown fullcloth.

Father was an important man. He had a good farm. He drove the best horses in that country. His word was as good as his bond, and every year he put money in the bank. When Father

22

drove into Malone, all the townspeople spoke to him respectfully.

Royal came up with his milk-pail and the lantern. He said in a low voice:

"Father, Big Bill Ritchie came to school to-day."

The holes in the tin lantern freckled everything with little lights and shadows. Almanzo could see that Father looked solemn; he stroked his beard and slowly shook his head. Almanzo waited anxiously, but Father only took the lantern and made a last round of the barns to see that everything was snug for the night. Then they went to the house.

The cold was cruel. The night was black and still, and the stars were tiny sparkles in the sky. Almanzo was glad to get into the big kitchen, warm with fire and candle-light. He was very hungry.

Soft water from the rain-barrel was warming on the stove. First Father, then Royal, then Almanzo took his turn at the wash-basin on the bench by the door. Almanzo wiped on the linen

23

roller-towel, then standing before the little mirror on the wall he parted his wet hair and combed it smoothly down.

The kitchen was full of hoopskirts, balancing and swirling. Eliza Jane and Alice were hurrying to dish up supper. The salty brown smell of frying ham made Almanzo's stomach gnaw inside him.

He stopped just a minute in the pantry door. Mother was straining the milk, at the far end of the long pantry; her back was toward him. The shelves on both sides were loaded with good things to eat. Big yellow cheeses were stacked there, and large brown cakes of maple sugar, and there were crusty loaves of fresh-baked bread, and four large cakes, and one whole shelf full of pies. One of the pies was cut, and a little piece of crust was temptingly broken off; it would never be missed.

Almanzo hadn't even moved yet. But Eliza Jane cried out:

"Almanzo, you stop that! Mother!"

Mother didn't turn around. She said:

24

"Leave that be, Almanzo. You'll spoil your supper."

That was so senseless that it made Almanzo mad. One little bite couldn't spoil a supper. He was starving, and they wouldn't let him eat anything until they had put it on the table. There wasn't any sense in it. But of course he could not say this to Mother; he had to obey her without a word.

He stuck out his tongue at Eliza Jane. She couldn't do anything; her hands were full. Then he went quickly into the dining-room.

The lamplight was dazzling. By the square heating-stove set into the wall, Father was talking politics to Mr. Corse. Father's face was toward the supper table, and Almanzo dared not touch anything on it.

There were slabs of tempting cheese, there was a plate of quivering headcheese; there were glass dishes of jams and jellies and pre-

25

serves, and a tall pitcher of milk, and a steaming pan of baked beans with a crisp bit of fat pork in the crumbling brown crust.

Almanzo looked at them all, and something twisted in his middle. He swallowed, and went slowly away.

The dining-room was pretty. There were green stripes and rows of tiny red flowers on the chocolate-brown wall-paper, and Mother had woven the rag-carpet to match. She had dyed the rags green and chocolate-brown, and woven them in stripes, with a tiny stripe of red and white rags twisted together between them. The tall corner cupboards were full of fascinating things—sea-shells, and petrified wood, and curious rocks, and books. And over the center-table hung an air-castle. Alice had made it of clean yellow wheat-straws, set together airily, with bits of bright-colored cloth at the corners. It swayed and quivered in the slightest breath of air, and the lamplight ran gleaming along the golden straws.

But to Almanzo the most beautiful sight was

26

his mother, bringing in the big willow-ware platter full of sizzling ham.

Mother was short and plump and pretty. Her eyes were blue, and her brown hair was like a bird's smooth wings. A row of little red buttons ran down the front of her dress of wine-colored wool, from her flat white linen collar to the white apron tied round her waist. Her big sleeves hung like large red bells at either end of the blue platter. She came through the doorway with a little pause and a tug, because her hoop-skirts were wider than the door.

The smell of the ham was almost more than Almanzo could bear.

Mother set the platter on the table. She looked to see that everything was ready, and the table properly set. She took off her apron and hung it in the kitchen. She waited until Father had finished what he was saying to Mr. Corse. But at last she said,

"James, supper is ready."

It seemed a long time before they were all in

27

their places. Father sat at the head of the table, Mother at the foot. Then they must all bow their heads while Father asked God to bless the food. After that, there was a little pause before Father unfolded his napkin and tucked it in the neckband of his frock.

He began to fill the plates. First he filled Mr. Corse's plate. Then Mother's. Then Royal's and Eliza Jane's and Alice's. Then, at last, he filled Almanzo's plate.

"Thank you," Almanzo said. Those were the only words he was allowed to speak at table. Children must be seen and not heard. Father and Mother and Mr. Corse could talk, but Royal and Eliza Jane and Alice and Almanzo must not say a word.

Almanzo ate the sweet, mellow baked beans. He ate the bit of salt pork that melted like cream in his mouth. He ate mealy boiled potatoes, with brown ham-gravy. He ate the ham. He bit deep into velvety bread spread with sleek butter, and he ate the crisp golden crust. He demolished a tall heap of pale mashed turnips, and a hill of stewed yellow pumpkin. Then he sighed, and tucked his napkin deeper into the neckband of his red waist. And he ate plum preserves, and strawberry jam, and grape jelly, and spiced watermelon-rind pickles. He felt very comfortable inside. Slowly he ate a large piece of pumpkin pie.

He heard Father say to Mr. Corse:

"The Hardscrabble boys came to school today, Royal tells me."

"Yes," Mr. Corse said.

"I hear they're saying they'll throw you out."

Mr. Corse said, "I guess they'll be trying it."

Father blew on the tea in his saucer. He tasted it, then drained the saucer and poured a little more tea into it.

"They have driven out two teachers," he said. "Last year they hurt Jonas Lane so bad he died of it later."

"I know," Mr. Corse said. "Jonas Lane and I went to school together. He was my friend."

Father did not say any more.

Chapter 3

Winter Night

AFTER supper Almanzo took care of his moccasins. Every night he sat by the kitchen stove and rubbed them with tallow. He held them in the heat and rubbed the melting tallow into the leather with the palm of his hand. His moccasins would always be comfortably soft, and keep his feet dry, as long as the leather was well greased, and he didn't stop rubbing until it would absorb no more tallow.

Royal sat by the stove, too, and greased his boots. Almanzo couldn't have boots; he had to wear moccasins because he was a little boy.

Mother and the girls washed the dishes and swept the pantry and kitchen, and downstairs in the big cellar Father cut up carrots and potatoes to feed the cows next day.

When the work was done, Father came up the cellar stairs, bringing a big pitcher of sweet cider and a panful of apples. Royal took the corn-popper and a pannikin of popcorn. Mother banked the kitchen fire with ashes for the night, and when everyone else had left the kitchen she blew out the candles.

They all settled down cosily by the big stove in the dining-room wall. The back of the stove was in the parlor, where nobody went except when company came. It was a fine stove; it warmed the dining-room and the parlor, its chimney warmed the bedrooms upstairs, and its whole top was an oven.

Royal opened its iron door, and with the poker he broke the charred logs into a shimmering bed of coals. He put three handfuls of popcorn into the big wire popper, and shook the popper over the coals. In a little while a kernel popped, then another, then three or four at once, and all at once furiously the hundreds of little pointed kernels exploded.

When the big dishpan was heaping full of fluffy white popcorn, Alice poured melted butter over it, and stirred and salted it. It was hot and crackling crisp, and deliciously buttery and salty, and everyone could eat all he wanted to.

Mother knitted and rocked in her high-backed rocking-chair. Father carefully scraped a new ax-handle with a bit of broken glass. Royal carved a chain of tiny links from a smooth stick of pine, and Alice sat on her hassock, doing her woolwork embroidery. And they all ate popcorn and apples, and drank sweet cider, except Eliza Jane. Eliza Jane read aloud the news in the New York weekly paper.

Almanzo sat on a footstool by the stove, an apple in his hand, a bowl of popcorn by his side, and his mug of cider on the hearth by his feet. He bit the juicy apple, then he ate some popcorn, then he took a drink of cider. He thought about popcorn.

Popcorn is American. Nobody but the Indians ever had popcorn, till after the Pilgrim Fathers came to America. On the first Thanksgiving Day, the Indians were invited to dinner, and they came, and they poured out on the table a big bagful of popcorn. The Pilgrim Fathers didn't know what it was. The Pilgrim Mothers didn't know, either. The Indians had popped it, but probably it wasn't very good. Probably they didn't butter it or salt it, and it would be cold and tough after they had carried it around in a bag of skins.

Almanzo looked at every kernel before he ate it. They were all different shapes. He had eaten thousands of handfuls of popcorn, and never found two kernels alike. Then he thought that if he had some milk, he would have popcorn and milk.

You can fill a glass full to the brim with milk, and fill another glass of the same size brim full of popcorn, and then you can put all the popcorn kernel by kernel into the milk, and the milk will not run over. You cannot do this with bread. Popcorn and milk are the only two things that will go into the same place.

Then, too, they are good to eat. But Almanzo was not very hungry, and he knew Mother would not want the milkpans disturbed. If you disturb milk when the cream is rising, the cream will not be so thick. So Almanzo ate another apple and drank cider with his popcorn and did not say anything about popcorn and milk.

When the clock struck nine, that was bed-time. Royal laid away his chain and Alice her woolwork. Mother stuck her needles in her ball of yarn, and Father wound the tall clock. He put another log in the stove and closed the dampers.

"It's a cold night," Mr. Corse said.

"Forty below zero," said Father, "and it will be colder before morning."

Royal lighted a candle and Almanzo followed him sleepily to the stairway door. The cold on the stairs made him wide awake at once. He ran clattering upstairs. The bedroom was so cold that he could hardly unbutton his clothes and put on his long woolen nightshirt and nightcap. He should have knelt down to say his prayers, but he didn't. His nose ached with cold and his teeth were chattering. He dived into the soft goose-feather bed, between the blankets, and pulled the covers over his nose.

The next thing he knew, the tall clock down-stairs was striking twelve. The darkness pressed

35

his eyes and forehead, and it seemed full of little prickles of ice. He heard someone move downstairs, then the kitchen door opened and shut. He knew that Father was going to the barn.

Even those great barns could not hold all Father's wealth of cows and oxen and horses and hogs and calves and sheep. Twenty-five young cattle had to sleep under a shed in the barnyard. If they lay still all night, on nights as cold as this, they would freeze in their sleep. So at midnight, in the bitter cold, Father got out of his warm bed and went to wake them up.

Out in the dark, cold night, Father was rousing up the young cattle. He was cracking his whip and running behind them, around and around the barnyard. He would run and keep them galloping till they were warmed with exercise.

Almanzo opened his eyes again, and the candle was sputtering on the bureau. Royal was dressing. His breath froze white in the air. The candlelight was dim, as though the darkness were trying to put it out.

36

Suddenly Royal was gone, the candle was not there, and Mother was calling from the foot of the stairs:

"Almanzo! What's the matter? Be you sick? It's five o'clock!"

He crawled out, shivering. He pulled on his trousers and waist, and ran downstairs to button up by the kitchen stove. Father and Royal had gone to the barns. Almanzo took the milk-pails and hurried out. The night seemed very large and still, and the stars sparkled like frost in the black sky.

When the chores were done and he came back with Father and Royal to the warm kitchen, breakfast was almost ready. How good it smelled! Mother was frying pancakes, and the big blue platter, keeping hot on the stove's hearth, was full of plump brown sausage cakes in their brown gravy.

Almanzo washed as quickly as he could, and combed his hair. As soon as Mother finished straining the milk, they all sat down and Father asked the blessing for breakfast.

37

There was oatmeal with plenty of thick cream and maple sugar. There were fried potatoes, and the golden buckwheat cakes, as many as Almanzo wanted to eat, with sausages and gravy or with butter and maple syrup. There were preserves and jams and jellies and doughnuts. But best of all Almanzo liked the spicy apple pie, with its thick, rich juice and its crumbly crust. He ate two big wedges of the pie.

Then, with his cap's warm ear-muffs over his ears, and his muffler wrapped up to his nose, and the dinner-pail in his mittened hand, he started down the long road to another day at school.

He did not want to go. He did not want to be there when the big boys thrashed Mr. Corse. But he had to go to school because he was almost nine years old.

Chapter 4

Surprise

EVERY day at noon the wood-haulers came down Hardscrabble Hill, and the boys hitched their sleds to the bobsleds' runners and rode away down the road. But they went only a little way, and came back in time. Only Big Bill Ritchie and his friends didn't care how soon Mr. Corse tried to punish them.

One day they were gone until after recess. When they came tramping into the schoolhouse they all grinned impudently at Mr. Corse. He waited until they were in their seats. Then he stood up, pale, and he said:

"If this occurs again, I shall punish you."

Everybody knew what would happen next day.

When Royal and Almanzo reached home that night, they told Father. Almanzo said it wasn't fair. Mr. Corse wasn't big enough to fight even one of those big boys, and they would all jump on him at once.

"I wish I was big enough to fight 'em!" he said.

"Son, Mr. Corse hired out to teach the school," Father answered. "The school trustees were fair and aboveboard with him; they told him what he was undertaking. He undertook it. It's his job, not yours."

"But maybe they'll kill him!" Almanzo said.

"That's his business," said Father. "When a man undertakes a job, he has to stick to it till he finishes it. If Corse is the man I think he is, he'd thank nobody for interfering."

Almanzo couldn't help saying again: "It isn't fair. He can't fight all five of them."

40

"I wouldn't wonder if you'd be surprised, son," Father said. "Now you boys get a hustle on; these chores can't wait all night."

So Almanzo went to work and did not say any more.

All next morning, while he sat holding up his primer, he could not study. He was dreading what was going to happen to Mr. Corse. When the primer class was called, he could not read the lesson. He had to stay in with the girls at recess, and he wished he could lick Bill Ritchie.

At noon he went out to play, and he saw Mr. Ritchie, Bill's father, coming down the hill on his loaded bobsled. All the boys stood where they were and watched Mr. Ritchie. He was a big, rough man, with a loud voice and a loud laugh. He was proud of Bill because Bill could thrash school-teachers and break up the school.

Nobody ran to fasten a sled behind Mr. Ritchie's bobsled, but Bill and the other big boys climbed up on his load of wood. They rode, loudly talking, around the bend of the road and

41

out of sight. The other boys did not play any more; they stood and talked about what would happen.

When Mr. Corse rapped on the window, they went in soberly and soberly sat down.

That afternoon nobody knew the lessons. Mr. Corse called up class after class, and they lined up with their toes on a crack in the floor, but they could not answer his questions. Mr. Corse did not punish anybody. He said:

"We will have the same lesson again to-morrow."

Everybody knew that Mr. Corse would not be there tomorrow. One of the little girls began to cry, then three or four of them put their heads down on their desks and sobbed. Almanzo had to sit still in his seat and look at his primer.

After a long time Mr. Corse called him to the desk, to see if he could read the lesson now. Almanzo knew every word of it, but there was a lump in his throat that would not let the words out. He stood looking at the page while Mr. Corse waited. Then they heard the big boys coming.

Mr. Corse stood up and put his thin hand gently on Almanzo's shoulder. He turned him around and said:

"Go to your seat, Almanzo."

The room was still. Everybody was waiting. The big boys came up the path and clattered into the entry, hooting and jostling one another. The door banged open, and Big Bill Ritchie swaggered in. The other big boys were behind him.

Mr. Corse looked at them and did not say anything. Bill Ritchie laughed in his face, and still he did not speak. The big boys jostled Bill, and he jeered again at Mr. Corse. Then he led them all tramping loudly down the aisle to their seats.

Mr. Corse lifted the lid of his desk and dropped one hand out of sight behind the raised lid. He said:

"Bill Ritchie, come up here."

Big Bill jumped up and tore off his coat, yelling:

"Come on, boys!" He rushed up the aisle.

43

Almanzo felt sick inside; he didn't want to watch, but he couldn't help it.

Mr. Corse stepped away from his desk. His hand came from behind the desk lid, and a long, thin, black streak hissed through the air.

It was a blacksnake ox-whip fifteen feet long. Mr. Corse held the short handle, loaded with iron, that could kill an ox. The thin, long lash coiled around Bill's legs, and Mr. Corse jerked. Bill lurched and almost fell. Quick as black lightning the lash circled and struck and coiled again, and again Mr. Corse jerked.

"Come up here, Bill Ritchie," he said, jerking Bill toward him, and backing away.

Bill could not reach him. Faster and faster the lash was hissing and crackling, coiling and jerking, and more and more quickly Mr. Corse backed away, jerking Bill almost off his feet. Up and down they went in the open space in front of the desk. The lash kept coiling and tripping Bill, Mr. Corse kept running backward and striking.

Bill's trousers were cut through, his shirt was

44

slashed, his arms bleeding from the bite of the lash. It came and went, hissing, too fast to be seen. Bill rushed, and the floor shook when the whiplash jerked him over backwards. He got up swearing and tried to reach teacher's chair, to throw it. The lash jerked him around. He began

to bawl like a calf. He blubbered and begged.

The lash kept on hissing, circling, jerking. Bit by bit it jerked Bill to the door. Mr. Corse threw him headlong into the entry and slammed and locked the door. Turning quickly, he said,

"Now, John, come on up."

John was in the aisle, staring. He whirled around and tried to get away, but Mr. Corse took a quick step, caught him with the whiplash and jerked him forward.

"Oh, please, please, please, teacher!" John begged. Mr. Corse did not answer. He was panting and sweat trickled down his cheek. The whiplash was coiling and hissing, jerking John to the door. Mr. Corse threw him out and slammed the door, and turned.

The other big boys had got the window open. One, two, three, they jumped out into the deep snow and floundered away.

Mr. Corse coiled the whip neatly and laid it in his desk. He wiped his face with his handkerchief, straightened his collar, and said:

"Royal, will you please close the window?"

Royal tiptoed to the window and shut it. Then Mr. Corse called the arithmetic class. Nobody knew the lesson. All the rest of the afternoon, no one knew a lesson. And there was no recess that afternoon. Everybody had forgotten it.

Almanzo could hardly wait till school was dismissed and he could rush out with the other boys and yell. The big boys were licked! Mr. Corse had licked Bill Ritchie's gang from Hardscrabble Settlement!

But Almanzo did not know the best part of it till he listened to his father talking to Mr. Corse that night at supper.

"The boys didn't throw you out, Royal tells me," Father said.

"No," said Mr. Corse. "Thanks to your blacksnake whip."

Almanzo stopped eating. He sat and looked at Father. Father had known, all the time. It was Father's blacksnake whip that had bested Big Bill Ritchie. Almanzo was sure that Father

47

was the smartest man in the world, as well as the biggest and strongest.

Father was talking. He said that while the big boys were riding on Mr. Ritchie's bobsled they had told Mr. Ritchie that they were going to thrash the teacher that afternoon. Mr. Ritchie thought it was a good joke. He was so sure the boys would do it that he told everyone in town they had done it, and on his way home he stopped to tell Father that Bill had thrashed Mr. Corse and broken up the school again.

Almanzo thought how surprised Mr. Ritchie must have been when he got home and saw Bill.

Chapter 5

Birthday

NEXT morning while Almanzo was eating his oatmeal, Father said this was his birthday. Almanzo had forgotten it. He was nine years old, that cold winter morning.

"There's something for you in the wood-shed," Father said.

Almanzo wanted to see it right away. But Mother said if he did not eat his breakfast he was sick, and must take medicine. Then he ate as fast as he could, and she said:

"Don't take such big mouthfuls."

Mothers always fuss about the way you eat. You can hardly eat any way that pleases them.

But at last breakfast was over and Almanzo got to the woodshed. There was a little calf-yoke! Father had made it of red cedar, so it was strong and yet light. It was Almanzo's very own, and Father said,

"Yes, son, you are old enough now to break the calves."

Almanzo did not go to school that day. He did not have to go to school when there were more important things to do. He carried the little yoke to the barn, and Father went with him. Almanzo thought that if he handled the calves perfectly, perhaps Father might let him help with the colts next year.

Star and Bright were in their warm stall in the South Barn. Their little red sides were sleek and silky from all the curryings Almanzo had given them. They crowded against him when he went into the stall, and licked at him with their wet, rough tongues. They thought he had

50

brought them carrots. They did not know he was going to teach them how to behave like big oxen.

Father showed him how to fit the yoke carefully to their soft necks. He must scrape its inside curves with a bit of broken glass, till the yoke fitted perfectly and the wood was silky-smooth. Then Almanzo let down the bars of the stall, and the wondering calves followed him into the dazzling, cold, snowy barnyard.

Father held up one end of the yoke while Almanzo laid the other end on Bright's neck. Then Almanzo lifted up the bow under Bright's throat and pushed its ends through the holes made for them in the yoke. He slipped a wooden bow-pin through one end of the bow, above the yoke, and it held the bow in place.

Bright kept twisting his head and trying to see the strange thing on his neck. But Almanzo had made him so gentle that he stood quietly, and Almanzo gave him a piece of carrot.

Star heard him crunching it and came to get

51

his share. Father pushed him around beside
Bright, under the other end of the yoke, and
Almanzo pushed the other bow up under his
throat and fastened it with its bow-pin. There,
already, he had his little yoke of oxen.

Then Father tied a rope around Star's nubs
of horns and Almanzo took the rope. He stood
in front of the calves and shouted,

"Giddap!"

Star's neck stretched out longer and longer.

Almanzo pulled, till finally Star stepped forward. Bright snorted and pulled back. The yoke twisted Star's head around and stopped him, and the two calves stood wondering what it was all about.

Father helped Almanzo push them, till they stood properly side by side again. Then he said,

"Well, son, I'll leave you to figure it out." And he went into the barn.

Then Almanzo knew that he was really old enough to do important things all by himself.

He stood in the snow and looked at the calves, and they stared innocently at him. He wondered how to teach them what "Giddap!" meant. There wasn't any way to tell them. But he must find some way to tell them,

"When I say, 'Giddap!' you must walk straight ahead."

Almanzo thought awhile, and then he left the calves and went to the cows' feed-box, and filled his pockets with carrots. He came back and stood as far in front of the calves as he could, holding the rope in his left hand. He put his

53

right hand into the pocket of his barn jumper. Then he shouted, "Giddap!" and he showed Star and Bright a carrot in his hand.

They came eagerly.

"Whoa!" Almanzo shouted when they reached him, and they stopped for the carrot. He gave each of them a piece, and when they had eaten it he backed away again, and putting his hand in his pocket he shouted:

"Giddap!"

It was astonishing how quickly they learned that "Giddap!" meant to start forward, and "Whoa!" meant to stop. They were behaving as well as grown-up oxen when Father came to the barn door and said:

"That's enough, son."

Almanzo did not think it was enough, but of course he could not contradict Father.

"Calves will get sullen and stop minding you if you work them too long at first," Father said. "Besides, it's dinner-time."

Almanzo could hardly believe it. The whole morning had gone in a minute.

54

He took out the bow-pins, let the bows down, and lifted the yoke off the calves' necks. He put Star and Bright in their warm stall. Then Father showed him how to wipe the bows and yoke with wisps of clean hay, and hang them on their pegs. He must always clean them and keep them dry, or the calves would have sore necks.

In the Horse Barn he stopped just a minute to look at the colts. He liked Star and Bright, but calves were clumsy and awkward compared with the slender, fine, quick colts. Their nostrils fluttered when they breathed, their ears moved as swiftly as birds. They tossed their heads with a flutter of manes, and daintily pawed with their slender legs and little hoofs, and their eyes were full of spirit.

"I'd like to help break a colt," Almanzo ventured to say.

"It's a man's job, son," Father said. "One little mistake'll ruin a fine colt."

Almanzo did not say any more. He went soberly into the house.

It was strange to be eating all alone with

55

Father and Mother. They ate at the table in the kitchen, because there was no company today. The kitchen was bright with the glitter of snow outside. The floor and the tables were scrubbed bone white with lye and sand. The tin saucepans glittered silver, and the copper pots gleamed gold on the walls, the teakettle hummed, and the geraniums on the window-sill were redder than Mother's red dress.

Almanzo was very hungry. He ate in silence, busily filling the big emptiness inside him, while Father and Mother talked. When they finished eating, Mother jumped up and began putting the dishes into the dishpan.

"You fill the wood-box, Almanzo," she said. "And then there's other things you can do."

Almanzo opened the woodshed door by the stove. There, right before him, was a new hand-sled!

He could hardly believe it was for him. The calf-yoke was his birthday present. He asked:

"Whose sled is that, Father? Is it—it isn't for me?"

Mother laughed and Father twinkled his eyes and asked, "Do you know any other nine-year-old that wants it?"

It was a beautiful sled. Father had made it of hickory. It was long and slim and swift-looking; the hickory runners had been soaked and bent into long, clean curves that seemed ready to fly. Almanzo stroked the shiny-smooth wood. It was polished so perfectly that he could not feel even the tops of the wooden pegs that held it together. There was a bar between the runners, for his feet.

"Get along with you!" Mother said, laughing. "Take that sled outdoors where it belongs."

The cold stood steadily at forty below zero, but the sun was shining, and all afternoon Almanzo played with his sled. Of course it would not slide in the soft, deep snow, but in the road the bobsleds' runners had made two sleek, hard tracks. At the top of the hill Almanzo started the sled and flung himself on it, and away he went.

Only the track was curving and narrow, so sooner or later he spilled into the drifts. End over end went the flying sled, and headlong went Almanzo. But he floundered out, and climbed the hill again.

Several times he went into the house for apples and doughnuts and cookies. Downstairs was still warm and empty. Upstairs there was the thud-thud of Mother's loom and the clickety-clack of the flying shuttle. Almanzo opened the woodshed door and heard the slithery, soft sound of a shaving-knife, and the flap of a turned shingle.

He climbed the stairs to Father's attic workroom. His snowy mittens hung by their string around his neck; in his right hand he held a doughnut, and in his left hand two cookies. He took a bite of doughnut and then a bite of cooky.

Father sat astraddle on the end of the shaving-bench, by the window. The bench slanted upward toward him, and at the top of the slant two pegs stood up. At his right hand was a pile of rough shingles which he had split with his ax from short lengths of oak logs.

He picked up a shingle, laid its end against the

pegs, and then drew the shaving-knife up its side. One stroke smoothed it, another stroke shaved the upper end thinner than the lower end. Father flipped the shingle over. Two strokes on that side, and it was done. Father laid it on the pile of finished shingles, and set another rough one against the pegs.

His hands moved smoothly and quickly. They did not stop even when he looked up and twinkled at Almanzo.

"Be you having a good time, son?" he asked.

"Father, can I do that?" said Almanzo.

Father slid back on the bench to make room in front of him. Almanzo straddled it, and crammed the rest of the doughnut into his mouth. He took the handles of the long knife in his hands and shaved carefully up the shingle. It wasn't as easy as it looked. So Father put his big hands over Almanzo's, and together they shaved the shingle smooth.

Then Almanzo turned it over, and they shaved the other side. That was all he wanted to do. He got off the bench and went in to see Mother.

Her hands were flying and her right foot was tapping on the treadle of the loom. Back and forth the shuttle flew from her right hand to her left and back again, between the even threads of warp, and swiftly the threads of warp criss-crossed each other, catching fast the thread that the shuttle left behind it.

Thud! said the treadle. Clackety-clack! said the shuttle. Thump! said the hand-bar, and back flew the shuttle.

Mother's workroom was large and bright, and warm from the heating-stove's chimney. Mother's little rocking-chair was by one window, and beside it a basket of carpet-rags, torn for sewing. In a corner stood the idle spinning-wheel. All along one wall were shelves full of hanks of red and brown and blue and yellow yarn, which Mother had dyed last summer.

But the cloth on the loom was sheep's-gray. Mother was weaving undyed wool from a white sheep and wool from a black sheep, twisted together.

"What's that for?" said Almanzo.

"Don't point, Almanzo," Mother said. "That's not good manners." She spoke loudly, above the noise of the loom.

"Who is it for?" asked Almanzo, not pointing this time.

"Royal. It's his Academy suit," said Mother. Royal was going to the Academy in Malone next winter, and Mother was weaving the cloth for his new suit.

So everything was snug and comfortable in the house, and Almanzo went downstairs and took two more doughnuts from the doughnut-jar, and then he played outdoors again with his sled.

Too soon the shadows slanted down the eastward slopes, and he had to put his sled away and help water the stock, for it was chore-time.

The well was quite a long way from the barns. A little house stood over the pump, and the water ran down a trough through the wall and into the big watering-trough outside. The troughs were coated with ice, and the pump handle was so cold that it burned like fire if you touched it with a bare finger.

Boys sometimes dared other boys to lick a pump handle in cold weather. Almanzo knew better than to take the dare. Your tongue would freeze to the iron, and you must either starve to death or pull away and leave part of your tongue there.

Almanzo stood in the icy pumphouse and he pumped with all his might, while Father led the horses to the trough outside. First Father led out the teams, with the young colts following their mothers. Then he led out the older colts, one at a time. They were not yet well broken, and they pranced and jumped and jerked at the halter-rope, because of the cold. But Father hung on and did not let them get away.

All the time Almanzo was pumping as fast as he could. The water gushed from the pump with a chilly sound, and the horses thrust their shivering noses into it and drank it up quickly.

Then Father took the pump handle. He

63

pumped the big trough full, and he went to the barns and turned out all the cattle.

Cattle did not have to be led to water. They came eagerly to the trough and drank while Almanzo pumped, then they hurried back to the warm barns, and each went to its own place. Each cow turned into her own stall and put her head between her own stanchions. They never made a mistake.

Whether this was because they had more sense than horses, or because they had so little sense that they did everything by habit, Father did not know.

Now Almanzo took the pitchfork and began to clean the stalls, while Father measured oats and peas into the feed-boxes. Royal came from school, and they all finished the chores together as usual. Almanzo's birthday was over.

He thought he must go to school next day. But that night Father said it was time to cut ice. Almanzo could stay at home to help, and so could Royal.

Chapter 6

Filling the Ice-House

T H E weather was so cold that the snow was like sand underfoot. A little water thrown into the air came down as tiny balls of ice. Even on the south side of the house at noon the snow did not soften. This was perfect weather for cutting ice, because when the blocks were lifted from the pond, no water would drip; it would instantly freeze.

The sun was rising, and all the eastern slopes of the snowdrifts were rosy in its light, when Almanzo snuggled under the fur robes between

65

Father and Royal in the big bobsled, and they set out to the pond on Trout River.

The horses trotted briskly, shaking jingles from their bells. Their breaths steamed from their nostrils, and the bobsled's runners squeaked on the hard snow. The cold air crinkled inside Almanzo's tingling nose, but every minute the sun shone more brightly, striking tiny glitters of red and green light from the snow, and all through the woods there were sparkles of sharp white lights in icicles.

It was a mile to the pond in the woods, and once Father got out to put his hands over the horses' noses. Their breaths had frozen over their nostrils, making it hard for them to breathe. Father's hands melted the frost, and they went on briskly.

French Joe and Lazy John were waiting on the pond when the bobsled drove up. They were Frenchmen who lived in little log houses in the woods. They had no farms. They hunted and trapped and fished, they sang and joked and danced, and they drank red wine instead of cider. When Father needed a hired man, they worked for him and he paid them with salt pork from the barrels down cellar.

They stood on the snowy pond, in their tall boots and plaid jackets and fur caps with fur ear-muffs, and the frost of their breaths was on their long mustaches. Each had an ax on his shoulder, and they carried cross-cut saws.

A cross-cut saw has a long, narrow blade, with wooden handles at the ends. Two men must pull it back and forth across the edge of whatever they want to saw in two. But they could not saw ice that way, because the ice was solid underfoot, like a floor. It had no edge to saw across.

When Father saw them he laughed and called out:

"You flipped that penny yet?"

Everybody laughed but Almanzo. He did not know the joke. So French Joe told him:

"Once two Irishmen were sent out to saw ice with a cross-cut saw. They had never sawed ice before. They looked at the ice and they looked

67

at the saw, till at last Pat took a penny out of his pocket and he says, says he,

"'Now Jamie, be fair. Heads or tails, who goes below?'"

Then Almanzo laughed, to think of anyone going down into the dark, cold water under the ice, to pull one end of the cross-cut saw. It was funny that there were people who didn't know how to saw ice.

He trudged with the others across the ice to the middle of the pond. A sharp wind blew there, driving wisps of snow before it. Above the deep water the ice was smooth and dark, swept almost bare of snow. Almanzo watched while Joe and John chopped a big, three-cornered hole in it. They lifted out the broken pieces of ice and carried them away, leaving the hole full of open water.

"She's about twenty inches thick," Lazy John said.

"Then saw the ice twenty inches," said Father.

Lazy John and French Joe knelt at the edge

of the hole. They lowered their cross-cut saws into the water and began to saw. Nobody pulled the ends of the saws under water.

Side by side, they sawed two straight cracks through the ice, twenty inches apart, and twenty feet long. Then with the ax John broke the ice across, and a slab twenty inches wide, twenty inches thick, and twenty feet long rose a little and floated free.

With a pole John pushed the slab toward the three-cornered hole, and as the end was thrust out, crackling the thin ice freezing on the water, Joe sawed off twenty-inch lengths of it. Father picked up the cubes with the big iron ice-tongs, and loaded them on the bobsled.

Almanzo ran to the edge of the hole, watching the saw. Suddenly, right on the very edge, he slipped.

He felt himself falling headlong into the dark water. His hands couldn't catch hold of anything. He knew he would sink and be drawn under the solid ice. The swift current would pull him under the ice, where nobody could find him.

He'd drown, held down by the ice in the dark.

French Joe grabbed him just in time. He heard a shout and felt a rough hand jerk him by one leg, he felt a terrific crash, and then he was lying on his stomach on the good, solid ice. He got up on his feet. Father was coming, running.

Father stood over him, big and terrible.

"You ought to have the worst whipping of your life," Father said.

"Yes, Father," Almanzo whispered. He knew it. He knew he should have been more careful. A boy nine years old is too big to do foolish things because he doesn't stop to think. Almanzo knew that, and felt ashamed. He shrank up small inside his clothes and his legs shivered, afraid of the whipping. Father's whippings hurt. But he knew he deserved to be whipped. The whip was on the bobsled.

"I won't thrash you this time," Father decided. "But see to it you stay away from that edge."

"Yes, Father," Almanzo whispered. He went away from the hole, and did not go near it again.

Father finished loading the bobsled. Then he spread the laprobes on top of the ice, and Almanzo rode on them with Father and Royal, back to the ice-house near the barns.

The ice-house was built of boards with wide cracks between. It was set high from the ground on wooden blocks, and looked like a big cage. Only the floor and the roof were solid. On the floor was a huge mound of sawdust, which

Father had hauled from the lumber-mill.

With a shovel Father spread the sawdust three inches thick on the floor. On this he laid the cubes of ice, three inches apart. Then he drove back to the pond, and Almanzo went to work with Royal in the ice-house.

They filled every crack between the cubes with sawdust, and tamped it down tightly with sticks. Then they shoveled the whole mound of sawdust on top of the ice, in a corner, and where it had been they covered the floor with cubes of ice and packed them in sawdust. Then they covered it all with sawdust three inches thick.

They worked as fast as they could, but before they finished, Father came with another load of ice. He laid down another layer of ice cubes three inches apart, and drove away, leaving them to fill every crevice tightly with sawdust, and spread sawdust over the top, and shovel the rest of the mound of sawdust up again.

They worked so hard that the exercise kept them warm, but long before noon Almanzo was hungrier than wolves. He couldn't stop work

long enough to run into the house for a doughnut. All of his middle was hollow, with a gnaw-
ing inside it.

He knelt on the ice, pushing sawdust into the
cracks with his mittened hands, and pounding
it down with a stick as fast as he could, and he
asked Royal,

"What would you like best to eat?"

They talked about spareribs, and turkey with
dressing, and baked beans, and crackling cornbread, and other good things. But Almanzo said
that what he liked most in the world was fried
apples'n'onions.

When, at last, they went in to dinner, there
on the table was a big dish of them! Mother
knew what he liked best, and she had cooked it
for him.

Almanzo ate four large helpings of apples'n'-
onions fried together. He ate roast beef and
brown gravy, and mashed potatoes and creamed
carrots and boiled turnips, and countless slices
of buttered bread with crab-apple jelly.

"It takes a great deal to feed a growing boy,"

73

Mother said. And she put a thick slice of birds'-nest pudding on his bare plate, and handed him the pitcher of sweetened cream speckled with nutmeg.

Almanzo poured the heavy cream over the apples nested in the fluffy crust. The syrupy brown juice curled up around the edges of the cream. Almanzo took up his spoon and ate every bit.

Then until chore-time he and Royal worked in the ice-house. All next day they worked, and all the next day. Just at dusk on the third day, Father helped them spread the last layer of sawdust over the topmost cubes of ice, in the peak of the ice-house roof. And that job was done.

Buried in sawdust, the blocks of ice would not melt in the hottest summer weather. One at a time they would be dug out, and Mother would make ice-cream and lemonade and cold egg-nog.

Chapter 7

Saturday Night

THAT night was Saturday night. All day,
long Mother had been baking, and when Almanzo went into the kitchen for the milkpails,
she was still frying doughnuts. The place was
full of their hot, brown smell, and the wheaty
smell of new bread, the spicy smell of cakes,
and the syrupy smell of pies.

Almanzo took the biggest doughnut from the
pan and bit off its crisp end. Mother was rolling
out the golden dough, slashing it into long strips,

75

rolling and doubling and twisting the strips. Her fingers flew; you could hardly see them. The strips seemed to twist themselves under her hands, and to leap into the big copper kettle of swirling hot fat.

Plump! they went to the bottom, sending up bubbles. Then quickly they came popping up, to float and slowly swell, till they rolled themselves over, their pale golden backs going into the fat and their plump brown bellies rising out of it.

They rolled over, Mother said, because they were twisted. Some women made a new-fangled shape, round, with a hole in the middle. But round doughnuts wouldn't turn themselves over. Mother didn't have time to waste turning doughnuts; it was quicker to twist them.

Almanzo liked baking-day. But he didn't like Saturday night. On Saturday night there was no cosy evening by the heater, with apples, popcorn, and cider. Saturday night was bath night.

After supper Almanzo and Royal again put

on their coats and caps and mufflers and mittens. They carried a tub from the washtub outdoors to the rain-water barrel.

Everything was ghostly with snow. The stars were frosty in the sky, and only a little faint light came from the candle in the kitchen.

The inside of the rain-water barrel was coated thick with ice, and in the center, where the ice was chopped every day to keep the barrel from bursting, the hole had grown smaller and smaller. Royal chopped at it, and when his hatchet went through with an oosy thud, the water welled up quickly, because the ice was squeezing it from all sides.

It's odd that water swells when it freezes. Everything else gets smaller in the cold.

Almanzo began dipping water and floating pieces of ice into the washtub. It was cold, slow work, dipping through the small hole, and he had an idea.

Long icicles hung from the kitchen eaves. At the top they were a solid piece of ice, then their

77

pointed tips hung down almost to the snow. Almanzo took hold of one and jerked, but only the tip broke off.

The hatchet had frozen to the porch floor where Royal had laid it, but Almanzo tugged it loose. He lifted it up in both hands and hit the icicles. An avalanche of ice came down with a splintering crash. It was a glorious noise.

"Hi, gimme!" Royal said, but Almanzo hit the icicles again; the noise was louder than before.

"You're bigger than I be; you hit 'em with your fists," Almanzo said. So Royal hit the icicles with both his fists; Almanzo hit them again with the hatchet. The noise was immense.

Almanzo yelled and Royal yelled and they hit more and more icicles. Big pieces of ice were flying all over the porch floor, and flying pieces pitted the snow. Along the eaves there was a gap as though the roof had lost some teeth.

Mother flung open the kitchen door.

"Mercy on us!" she cried. "Royal, Almanzo! Be you hurt?"

78

"No, Mother," Almanzo said, meekly.

"What is it? What be you doing?"

Almanzo felt guilty. But they had not really been playing when they had work to do.

"Getting ice for the bath water, Mother," he said.

"My land! Such a racket I never heard! Must you yell like Comanches?"

"No, Mother," Almanzo said.

Mother's teeth chattered in the cold, and she shut the door. Almanzo and Royal silently picked up the fallen icicles and silently filled the tub. It was so heavy they staggered when they carried it, and Father had to lift it onto the kitchen stove.

The ice melted while Almanzo greased his moccasins and Royal greased his boots. In the pantry Mother was filling the six-quart pan with boiled beans, putting in onions and peppers and the piece of fat pork, and pouring scrolls of molasses over all. Then Almanzo saw her open the flour barrels. She flung rye flour and cornmeal into the big yellow crock, and stirred in milk

79

and eggs and things, and poured the big baking-pan full of the yellow-gray rye'n'injun dough.

"You fetch the rye'n'injun, Almanzo; don't spill it," she said. She snatched up the pan of beans and Almanzo followed more slowly with the heavy pan of rye'n'injun. Father opened the big doors of the oven in the heater, and Mother slid the beans and the bread inside. They would slowly bake there, till Sunday dinner-time.

Then Almanzo was left alone in the kitchen, to take his bath. His clean underwear was hanging on a chair-back to air and warm. The wash-cloth and towel and the small wooden pannikin of soft-soap were on another chair. He brought another washtub from the woodshed and put it on the floor in front of the open oven-door.

He took off his waist and one pair of socks and his pants. Then he dipped some warm water from the tub on the stove into the tub on the floor. He took off his other pair of socks and his underwear, and his bare skin felt good in the heat from the oven. He toasted in the heat, and he thought he might just put on his clean under-

80

wear and not take a bath at all. But Mother would look, when he went into the dining-room.

So he stepped into the water. It covered his feet. With his fingers he dug some of the brown, slimy soft-soap from the pannikin and smeared it on the washcloth. Then he scrubbed himself well all over.

The water was warm around his toes, but it

felt cold on his body. His wet belly steamed in the heat from the oven, but his wet back shivered. And when he turned around, his back seemed to blister, but his front was very cold. So he washed as quickly as he could, and he dried himself and got into his warm underwaist and his woolly long drawers, and he put on his long woolen nightshirt.

Then he remembered his ears. He took the washcloth again, and he scrubbed his ears and the back of his neck. He put on his nightcap.

He felt very clean and good, and his skin felt sleek in the fresh, warm clothes. It was the Saturday-night feeling.

It was pleasant, but Almanzo didn't like it well enough to take a bath for it. If he could have had his way, he wouldn't have taken a bath till spring.

He did not have to empty his tub, because if he went outdoors after taking a bath he would catch cold. Alice would empty the tub and wash it before she bathed in it. Then Eliza Jane would empty Alice's, and Royal would empty Eliza

82

Jane's, and Mother would empty Royal's. Late at night, Father would empty Mother's, and take his bath, and next morning he would empty the tub for the last time.

Almanzo went into the dining-room in his clean, creamy-white underwear and socks and night-shirt and cap. Mother looked at him, and he went to her to be inspected.

She laid down her knitting and she looked at his ears and the back of his neck and she looked at his soapy-clean face, and she gave him a hug and a squeeze. "There! Run along with you to bed!"

He lighted a candle and he padded quickly up the cold stairs and blew out the candle and jumped into the soft, cold feather-bed. He began to say his prayers, but went to sleep before he finished them.

Chapter 8

Sunday

WHEN Almanzo trudged into the kitchen next morning with two brimming milk-pails, Mother was making stacked pancakes because this was Sunday.

The big blue platter on the stove's hearth was full of plump sausage cakes; Eliza Jane was cutting apple pies and Alice was dishing up the oatmeal, as usual. But the little blue platter stood hot on the back of the stove, and ten stacks of pancakes rose in tall towers on it.

Ten pancakes cooked on the smoking griddle, and as fast as they were done Mother added an-

84

other cake to each stack and buttered it lavishly and covered it with maple sugar. Butter and sugar melted together and soaked the fluffy pancakes and dripped all down their crisp edges.

That was stacked pancakes. Almanzo liked them better than any other kind of pancakes.

Mother kept on frying them till the others had eaten their oatmeal. She could never make too many stacked pancakes. They all ate pile after pile of them, and Almanzo was still eating when Mother pushed back her chair and said,

"Mercy on us! eight o'clock! I must fly!"

Mother always flew. Her feet went pattering, her hands moved so fast you could hardly watch them. She never sat down in the daytime, except at her spinning-wheel or loom, and then her hands flew, her feet tapped, the spinning-wheel was a blur or the loom was clattering, thump! thud! clickety-clack! But on Sunday morning she made everybody else hurry, too.

Father curried and brushed the sleek brown driving-horses till they shone. Almanzo dusted the sleigh and Royal wiped the silver-mounted harness. They hitched up the horses, and then

85

they went to the house to put on their Sunday clothes.

Mother was in the pantry, setting the top crust on the Sunday chicken pie. Three fat hens were in the pie, under the bubbling gravy. Mother spread the crust and crimped the edges, and the gravy showed through the two pine-trees she had cut in the dough. She put the pie in the heating-stove's oven, with the beans and the rye'n'injun bread. Father filled the stove with hickory logs and closed the dampers, while Mother flew to lay out his clothes and dress herself.

Poor people had to wear homespun on Sundays, and Royal and Almanzo wore fullcloth. But Father and Mother and the girls were very fine, in clothes that Mother had made of store-boughten cloth, woven by machines.

She had made Father's suit of fine black broadcloth. The coat had a velvet collar, and his shirt was made of French calico. His stock was black silk, and on Sundays he did not wear boots; he wore shoes of thin calfskin.

Mother was dressed in brown merino, with a white lace collar, and white lace frills at her wrists, under the big, bell-shaped sleeves. She had knitted the lace of finest thread, and it was like cobwebs. There were rows of brown velvet around her sleeves and down the front of her basque, and she had made her bonnet of the same brown velvet, with brown velvet strings tied under her chin.

Almanzo was proud of Mother in her fine Sunday clothes. The girls were very fine, too, but he did not feel the same about them.

Their hoopskirts were so big that Royal and Almanzo could hardly get into the sleigh. They had to scrooge down and let those hoops bulge over their knees. And if they even moved, Eliza Jane would cry out: "Be careful, clumsy!"

And Alice would mourn:

"Oh dear me, my ribbons are mussed!"

But when they were all tucked under the buffalo-skin robes, with hot bricks at their feet, Father let the prancing horses go, and Almanzo forgot everything else.

The sleigh went like the wind. The beautiful horses shone in the sun; their necks were arched and their heads were up and their slender legs spurned the snowy road. They seemed to be flying, their glossy long manes and tails blown back in the wind of their speed.

Father sat straight and proud, holding the reins and letting the horses go as fast as they would. He never used the whip; his horses were gentle and perfectly trained. He had only to tighten or slacken the reins, and they obeyed him. His horses were the best horses in New York State, or maybe in the whole world. Malone was five miles away, but Father never started till thirty minutes before church-time.

That team would trot the whole five miles, and he would stable them and blanket them and be on the church steps when the bell rang.

When Almanzo thought that it would be years and years before he could hold the reins and drive horses like that, he could hardly bear it.

In no time at all, Father was driving into the church sheds in Malone. The sheds were one long, low building, all around the four sides of a square. You drove into the square through a gate. Every man who belonged to the church paid rent for a shed, according to his means, and Father had the best one. It was so large that he drove inside it to unhitch, and there was a manger with feed-boxes, and space for hay and oats.

Father let Almanzo help put blankets on the horses, while Mother and the girls shook out their skirts and smoothed their ribbons. Then they all walked sedately into the church. The first clang of the bell rang out when they were on the steps.

After that there was nothing to do but sit still till the sermon was over. It was two hours long. Almanzo's legs ached and his jaw wanted to yawn, but he dared not yawn or fidget. He must sit perfectly still and never take his eyes from the preacher's solemn face and wagging beard. Almanzo couldn't understand how Father knew that he wasn't looking at the preacher, if Father was looking at the preacher himself. But Father always did know.

At last it was over. In the sunshine outside the church, Almanzo felt better. Boys must not run or laugh or talk loudly on Sunday, but they could talk quietly, and Almanzo's cousin Frank was there.

Frank's father was Uncle Wesley; he owned the potato-starch mill and lived in town. He did not have a farm. So Frank was only a town boy and he played with town boys. But this Sunday morning he was wearing a store-boughten cap.

It was made of plaid cloth, machine-woven, and it had ear-flaps that buttoned under the chin. Frank unbuttoned them, and showed Almanzo that they would turn up and button across the cap's top. He said the cap came from New York City. His father had bought it in Mr. Case's store.

Almanzo had never seen a cap like that. He wanted one.

Royal said it was a silly cap. He said to Frank:

"What's the sense of ear-flaps that button over the top? Nobody has ears on top of his head." So Almanzo knew that Royal wanted a cap like that, too.

"How much did it cost?" Almanzo asked.

"Fifty cents," Frank said, proudly.

Almanzo knew he could not have one. The caps that Mother made were snug and warm, and it would be a foolish waste of money to buy a cap. Fifty cents was a lot of money.

"You just ought to see our horses," he said to Frank.

"Huh! they're not your horses!" Frank said. "They're your father's horses. You haven't got a horse, nor even a colt."

"I'm going to have a colt," said Almanzo.

"When?" Frank asked.

Just then Eliza Jane called over her shoulder: "Come, Almanzo! Father's hitching up!"

He hurried away after Eliza Jane, but Frank called after him, low:

"You are not either going to have a colt!"

Almanzo got soberly into the sleigh. He wondered if he would ever be big enough to have anything he wanted. When he was younger, Father sometimes let him hold the ends of the reins while Father drove, but he was not a baby now. He wanted to drive the horses, himself.

92

Father allowed him to brush and currycomb and rub down the gentle old work-horses, and to drive them on the harrow. But he could not even go into the stalls with the spirited driving-horses or the colts. He hardly dared stroke their soft noses through the bars, and scratch a little on their foreheads under the forelocks. Father said:

"You boys keep away from those colts. In five minutes you can teach them tricks it will take me months to gentle out of them."

He felt a little better when he sat down to the good Sunday dinner. Mother sliced the hot rye'n'injun bread on the bread-board by her plate. Father's spoon cut deep into the chicken-pie; he scooped out big pieces of thick crust and turned up their fluffy yellow under-sides on the plate. He poured gravy over them; he dipped up big pieces of tender chicken, dark meat and white meat sliding from the bones. He added a mound of baked beans and topped it with a quivering slice of fat pork. At the edge of the plate he piled dark-red beet pickles. And he handed the plate to Almanzo.

93

Silently Almanzo ate it all. Then he ate a piece of pumpkin pie, and he felt very full inside. But he ate a piece of apple pie with cheese.

After dinner Eliza Jane and Alice did the dishes, but Father and Mother and Royal and Almanzo did nothing at all. The whole afternoon they sat in the drowsy warm dining-room. Mother read the Bible and Eliza Jane read a book, and Father's head nodded till he woke with a jerk, and then it began to nod again. Royal fingered the wooden chain that he could not whittle, and Alice looked for a long time out of the window. But Almanzo just sat. He had to. He was not allowed to do anything else, for Sunday was not a day for working or playing. It was a day for going to church and for sitting still.

Almanzo was glad when it was time to do the chores.

Chapter 9

Breaking the Calves

ALMANZO had been so busy filling the ice-house that he had no time to give the calves another lesson. So on Monday morning he said:

"Father, I can't go to school today, can I? If I don't work those calves, they will forget how to act."

Father tugged his beard and twinkled his eyes.

"Seems as though a boy might forget his lesson, too," he said.

Almanzo had not thought of that. He thought a minute and said:

"Well, I have had more lessons than the calves, and besides, they are younger than I be."

Father looked solemn, but his beard had a smile under it, and Mother exclaimed:

"Oh, let the boy stay home if he wants! It won't hurt him for once in a way, and he's right, the calves do need breaking."

So Almanzo went to the barn and called the little calves out into the frosty air. He fitted the little yoke over their necks and he held up the bows and put the bow-pins in, and tied a rope around Star's small nubs of horns. He did this all by himself.

All that morning he backed, little by little, around the barnyard, shouting, "Giddap!" and then, "Whoa!" Star and Bright came eagerly when he yelled, "Giddap!" and they stopped when he said, "Whoa!" and licked up the pieces of carrot from his woolly mittens.

Now and then he ate a piece of raw carrot, himself. The outside part is best. It comes off in a thick, solid ring, and it is sweet. The inside part is juicier, and clear like yellow ice, but it has a thin, sharp taste.

At noon Father said the calves had been worked enough for one day, and that afternoon he would show Almanzo how to make a whip.

They went into the woods, and Father cut some moosewood boughs. Almanzo carried them up to Father's workroom over the woodshed, and Father showed him how to peel off the bark in strips, and then how to braid a whiplash. First he tied the ends of five strips together, and then he braided them in a round, solid braid.

All that afternoon he sat beside Father's bench. Father shaved shingles and Almanzo carefully braided his whip, just as Father braided the big blacksnake whips of leather. While he turned and twisted the strips, the thin outer bark fell off in flakes, leaving the soft, white, inside bark. The whip would have been white, except that Almanzo's hands left a few smudges.

He could not finish it before chore-time, and

97

the next day he had to go to school. But he braided his whip every evening by the heater, till the lash was five feet long. Then Father lent him his jack-knife, and Almanzo whittled a wooden handle, and bound the lash to it with strips of moosewood bark. The whip was done.

It would be a perfectly good whip until it dried brittle in the hot summer. Almanzo could crack it almost as loudly as Father cracked a blacksnake whip. And he did not finish it a minute too soon, for already he needed it to give the calves their next lesson.

Now he had to teach them to turn to the left when he shouted, "Haw!" and to turn to the right when he shouted, "Gee!"

As soon as the whip was ready, he began. Every Saturday morning he spent in the barnyard, teaching Star and Bright. He never whipped them; he only cracked the whip.

He knew you could never teach an animal anything if you struck it, or even shouted at it angrily. He must always be gentle, and quiet, and patient, even when they made mistakes.

Star and Bright must like him and trust him and know he would never hurt them, for if they were once afraid of him they would never be good, willing, hard-working oxen.

Now they always obeyed him when he shouted, "Giddap!" and "Whoa!" So he did not stand in front of them any longer. He stood at Star's left side. Star was next him, so Star was the nigh ox. Bright was on the other side of Star, so Bright was the off ox.

Almanzo shouted, "Gee!" and cracked the whip with all his might, close beside Star's head. Star dodged to get away from it, and that turned both calves to the right. Then Almanzo said, "Giddap!" and let them walk a little way, quietly.

Then he made the whip-lash curl in the air and crack loudly, on the other side of Bright, and with the crack he yelled, "Haw!"

Bright swerved away from the whip, and that turned both calves to the left.

Sometimes they jumped and started to run. Then Almanzo said, "Whoa!" in a deep, solemn voice like Father's. And if they didn't stop, he ran after them and headed them off. When that happened, he had to make them practice, "Giddap!" and "Whoa!" again, for a long time. He had to be very patient.

One very cold Saturday morning, when the calves were feeling frisky, they ran away the first time he cracked the whip. They kicked up their heels and ran bawling around the barnyard, and when he tried to stop them they ran right over him, tumbling him into the snow. They kept right on running because they liked to run. He could hardly do anything with them that morning. And he was so mad that he shook all over, and tears ran down his cheeks.

He wanted to yell at those mean calves, and kick them, and hit them over the head with the butt of his whip. But he didn't. He put up the whip, and he tied the rope again to Star's horns, and he made them go twice around the barnyard, starting when he said "Giddap!" and stopping when he said, "Whoa!"

Afterward he told Father about it, because he thought anyone who was as patient as that, with calves, was patient enough to be allowed at least to currycomb the colts. But Father didn't seem to think of that. All he said was:

"That's right, son. Slow and patient does it. Keep on that way, and you'll have a good yoke of oxen, yet."

The very next Saturday, Star and Bright obeyed him perfectly. He did not need to crack the whip, because they obeyed his shout. But he cracked it anyway; he liked to.

That Saturday the French boys, Pierre and Louis, came to see Almanzo. Pierre's father was Lazy John, and Louis' father was French Joe. They lived with many brothers and sisters in the little houses in the woods, and went fishing and hunting and berrying; they never had to go to school. But often they came to work or play with Almanzo.

They watched while Almanzo showed off his calves in the barnyard. Star and Bright were behaving so well that Almanzo had a splendid idea. He brought out his beautiful birthday hand-sled, and with an auger he bored a hole through the cross-piece between the runners in front. Then he took one of Father's chains, and a lynch-pin from Father's big bobsled, and he hitched up the calves.

There was a little iron ring underneath their yoke in the middle, just like the rings in big yokes. Almanzo stuck the handle of his sled through this ring, as far as the handle's little cross-piece. The cross-piece kept it from going too far through the ring. Then he fastened one end of the chain to the ring, and the other end he wound around the lynch-pin in the hole in the cross-bar, and fastened it.

When Star and Bright pulled, they would pull the sled by the chain. When they stopped, the sled's stiff handle would stop the sled.

"Now, Louis, you get on the sled," Almanzo said.

"No, I'm biggest!" Pierre said, pushing Louis back. "I get first ride."

"You better not," said Almanzo. "When the calves feel the heft, they're liable to run away. Let Louis go first because he's lighter."

"No, I don't want to," Louis said.

"I guess you better," Almanzo told him.

"No," said Louis.

"Be you scared?" Almanzo asked.

"Yes, he's scared," Pierre said.

"I am not scared," Louis said. "I just don't want to."

"He's scared," Pierre sneered.

"Yes, he's scared," Almanzo said.

Louis said he was not either scared.

"You are, too, scared," Almanzo and Pierre said. They said he was a fraidy-cat. They said he was a baby. Pierre told him to go back to his mamma. So finally Louis sat carefully on the sled.

Almanzo cracked his whip and shouted, "Giddap!"

Star and Bright started, and stopped. They tried to turn around to see what was behind them. But Almanzo sternly said, "Giddap!"

again, and this time they started and kept on going. Almanzo walked beside them, cracking his whip and shouting "Gee!" and he drove them clear around the barnyard. Pierre ran after the sled and got on, too, and still the calves behaved perfectly. So Almanzo opened the barnyard gate.

Pierre and Louis quickly got off the sled and Pierre said:

"They'll run away!"

Almanzo said, "I guess I know how to handle my own calves."

He went back to his place beside Star. He cracked his whip and shouted, "Giddap!" and he drove Star and Bright straight out of the safe barnyard into the big, wide, glittering world outside.

He shouted, "Haw!" and he shouted, "Gee!" and he drove them past the house. He drove them out to the road. They stopped when he shouted, "Whoa!"

Pierre and Louis were excited now. They piled onto the sled, but Almanzo made them

slide back. He was going to ride, too. He sat in front; Pierre held onto him, and Louis held onto Pierre. Their legs stuck out, and they held them stiffly up above the snow. Almanzo proudly cracked his whip and shouted, "Giddap!"

Up went Star's tail, up went Bright's tail, up went their heels. The sled bounced into the air, and then everything happened all at once.

"Baw-aw-aw!" said Star. "Baw-aw-aw-aw!"

said Bright. Right in Almanzo's face were flying hoofs and swishing tails, and close overhead were galumphing hindquarters. "Whoa!" yelled Almanzo. "Whoa!"

"Baw-aw!" said Bright. "Baw-aw-aw!" said Star. It was far swifter than sliding downhill. Trees and snow and calves' hindlegs were all mixed up. Every time the sled came down Almanzo's teeth crashed together.

Bright was running faster than Star. They were going off the road. The sled was turning over. Almanzo yelled, "Haw! Haw!" He went headlong into deep snow, yelling, "Haw!"

His open mouth was full of snow. He spit it out, and wallowed, scrambled up.

Everything was still. The road was empty. The calves were gone, the sled was gone. Pierre and Louis were coming up out of the snow. Louis was swearing in French, but Almanzo paid no attention to him. Pierre sputtered and wiped the snow from his face, and said:

"*Sacre bleu!* I think you say you drive your calves. They not run away, eh?"

Far down the road, almost buried in the deep drifts by the mound of snow over the stone fence, Almanzo saw the calves' red backs.

"They did not run away," he said to Pierre. "They only ran. There they be."

He went down to look at them. Their heads and their backs were above the snow. The yoke was crooked and their necks were askew in the bows. Their noses were together and their eyes were large and wondering. They seemed to be asking each other, "What happened?"

Pierre and Louis helped dig the snow away from them and the sled. Almanzo straightened the yoke and the chain. Then he stood in front of them and said, "Giddap!" while Pierre and Louis pushed them from behind. The calves climbed into the road, and Almanzo headed them toward the barn. They went willingly. Almanzo walked beside Star, cracking his whip and shouting, and everything he told them to do, they did. Pierre and Louis walked behind. They would not ride.

Almanzo put the calves in their stall and gave

them each a nubbin of corn. He wiped the yoke carefully and hung it up; he put the whip on its nail, and he wiped the chain and the lynch-pin and put them where Father had left them. Then he told Pierre and Louis that they could sit behind him, and they slid downhill on the sled till chore-time.

That night Father asked him:

"You have some trouble this afternoon, son?"

"No," Almanzo said. "I just found out I have to break Star and Bright to drive when I ride."

So he did that, in the barnyard.

Chapter 10

The Turn of the Year

T H E days were growing longer, but the cold was more intense. Father said:

> "When the days begin to lengthen
> The cold begins to strengthen."

At last the snow softened a little on the south and west slopes. At noon the icicles dripped. Sap was rising in the trees, and it was time to make sugar.

In the cold mornings just before sunrise, Almanzo and Father set out to the maple grove. Father had a big wooden yoke on his shoulders and Almanzo had a little yoke. From the ends of the yokes hung strips of moosewood bark, with large iron hooks on them, and a big wooden bucket swung from each hook.

In every maple tree Father had bored a small hole, and fitted a little wooden spout into it. Sweet maple sap was dripping from the spouts into small pails.

Going from tree to tree, Almanzo emptied the sap into his big buckets. The weight hung from his shoulders, but he steadied the buckets with his hands to keep them from swinging. When they were full, he went to the great cal-dron and emptied them into it.

The huge caldron hung from a pole set be-tween two trees. Father kept a bonfire blazing under it, to boil the sap.

Almanzo loved trudging through the frozen wild woods. He walked on snow that had never been walked on before, and only his own tracks followed behind him. Busily he emptied the little pails into the buckets, and whenever he was thirsty he drank some of the thin, sweet, icy-cold sap.

He liked to go back to the roaring fire. He poked it and saw the sparks fly. He warmed his face and hands in the scorching heat and smelled the sap boiling. Then he went into the woods again.

At noon all the sap was boiling in the caldron. Father opened the lunch-pail, and Almanzo sat on the log beside him. They ate and talked. Their feet were stretched out to the fire, and a pile of logs was at their backs. All around them were snow and ice and wild woods, but they were snug and cosy.

After they had eaten, Father stayed by the fire to watch the sap, but Almanzo hunted wintergreen berries.

Under the snow on the south slopes the bright-red berries were ripe among their thick green leaves. Almanzo took off his mittens and pawed away the snow with his bare hands. He found the red clusters and filled his mouth full.

The cold berries crunched between his teeth, gushing out their aromatic juice.

Nothing else was ever so good as wintergreen berries dug out of the snow.

Almanzo's clothes were covered with snow, his fingers were stiff and red with cold, but he never left a south slope until he had pawed it all over.

When the sun was low behind the maple-trunks, Father threw snow on the fire and it died in sizzles and steam. Then Father dipped the hot syrup into the buckets. He and Almanzo set their shoulders under the yokes again, and carried the buckets home.

They poured the syrup into Mother's big brass kettle on the cook-stove. Then Almanzo began the chores while Father fetched the rest of the syrup from the woods.

After supper, the syrup was ready to sugar off. Mother ladled it into six-quart milk-pans and left it to cool. In the morning every pan held a big cake of solid maple-sugar. Mother dumped out the round, golden-brown cakes and stored them on the top pantry shelves.

Day after day the sap was running, and every morning Almanzo went with Father to gather and boil it; every night Mother sugared it off. They made all the sugar they could use next year. Then the last boiling of syrup was not sugared off; it was stored in jugs down cellar, and that was the year's syrup.

When Alice came home from school she smelled Almanzo, and she cried out, "Oh, you've been eating wintergreen berries!"

She thought it wasn't fair that she had to go to school while Almanzo gathered sap and ate wintergreen berries. She said:

"Boys have all the fun."

She made Almanzo promise that he wouldn't touch the south slopes along Trout River, beyond the sheep pasture.

So on Saturdays they went together to paw over those slopes. When Almanzo found a red cluster he yelled, and when Alice found one she squealed, and sometimes they divided, and sometimes they didn't. But they went on their hands and knees all over those south slopes, and they ate wintergreen berries all afternoon.

Almanzo brought home a pailful of the thick, green leaves, and Alice crammed them into a big bottle. Mother filled the bottle with whisky and set it away. That was her wintergreen flavoring for cakes and cookies.

Every day the snow was melting a little. The cedars and spruces shook it off, and it fell in blobs from the bare branches of oaks and maples and beeches. All along the walls of barns and house the snow was pitted with water falling from the icicles, and finally the icicles fell crashing.

The earth showed in wet, dark patches here and there. The patches spread. Only the trodden paths were still white, and a little snow remained on the north sides of buildings and woodpiles. Then the winter term of school ended and spring had come.

One morning Father drove to Malone. Before noon he came hurrying home, and shouted the news from the buggy. The New York potato-buyers were in town!

Royal ran to help hitch the team to the

wagon, Alice and Almanzo ran to get bushel
baskets from the woodshed. They rolled them
bumpity-bump down the cellar stairs, and began
filling them with potatoes as fast as they could.
They filled two baskets before Father drove the
wagon to the kitchen porch.

Then the race began. Father and Royal hurried the baskets upstairs and dumped them into the wagon, and Almanzo and Alice hurried to fill more baskets faster than they were carried away.

Almanzo tried to fill more baskets than Alice, but he couldn't. She worked so fast that she was turning back to the bin while her hoopskirts were still whirling the other way. When she pushed back her curls, her hands left smudges on her cheeks. Almanzo laughed at her dirty face, and she laughed at him.

"Look at yourself in the glass! You're dirtier than I be!"

They kept the baskets full; Father and Royal never had to wait. When the wagon was full, Father drove away in a hurry.

It was mid-afternoon before he came back, but Royal and Almanzo and Alice filled the wagon again while he ate some cold dinner, and he hauled another load away. That night Alice helped Royal and Almanzo do the chores. Father was not there for supper; he did not come before bedtime. Royal sat up to wait for him. Late in the night Almanzo heard the wagon, and Royal went out to help Father curry and brush the tired horses who had done twenty miles of hauling that day.

The next morning, and the next, they all began loading potatoes by candlelight, and Father was gone with the first load before sunrise. On the third day the potato-train left for New York city. But all Father's potatoes were on it.

"Five hundred bushels at a dollar a bushel," he said to Mother at supper. "I told you when potatoes were cheap last fall that they'd be high in the spring."

That was five hundred dollars in the bank. They were all proud of Father, who raised such good potatoes and knew so well when to store them and when to sell them.

"That's pretty good," Mother said, beaming. They all felt happy. But later Mother said,

"Well, now that's off our hands, we'll start house-cleaning tomorrow, bright and early."

Almanzo hated house-cleaning. He had to pull

up carpet tacks, all around the edges of miles of carpet. Then the carpets were hung on clotheslines outdoors, and he had to beat them with a long stick. When he was little he had run under the carpets, playing they were tents. But now he was nine years old, he had to beat those carpets without stopping, till no more dust would come out of them.

Everything in the house was moved, everything was scrubbed and scoured and polished. All the curtains were down, all the feather-beds were outdoors, airing, all the blankets and quilts were washed. From dawn to dark Almanzo was running, pumping water, fetching wood, spreading clean straw on the scrubbed floors and then helping to stretch the carpets over it, and then tacking all those edges down again.

Days and days he spent in the cellar. He helped Royal empty the vegetable-bins. They sorted out every spoiled apple and carrot and turnip, and put back the good ones into a few bins that Mother had scrubbed. They took down the other bins and stored them in the woodshed.

118

They carried out crocks and jars and jugs, till the cellar was almost empty. Then Mother scrubbed the walls and floor. Royal poured water into pails of lime, and Almanzo stirred the lime till it stopped boiling and was whitewash. Then they whitewashed the whole cellar. That was fun.

"Mercy on us!" Mother said when they came upstairs. "Did you get as much whitewash on the cellar as you got on yourselves?"

The whole cellar was fresh and clean and snow-white when it dried. Mother moved her milk-pans down to the scrubbed shelves. The butter-tubs were scoured white with sand and dried in the sun, and Almanzo set them in a row on the clean cellar floor, to be filled with the summer's butter.

Outdoors the lilacs and the snowball bushes were in bloom. Violets and buttercups were blossoming in the green pastures, birds were building their nests, and it was time to work in the fields.

Chapter 11

Springtime

NOW breakfast was eaten before dawn, and the sun was rising beyond the dewy meadows when Almanzo drove his team from the barns.

He had to stand on a box to lift the heavy collars onto the horses' shoulders and to slip the bridles over their ears, but he knew how to drive. He had learned when he was little. Father wouldn't let him touch the colts, nor drive the spirited young horses, but now that he was old enough to work in the fields he could drive the

120

old, gentle work-team, Bess and Beauty.

They were wise, sober mares. When they were turned out to pasture they did not whinny and gallop like colts; they looked about them, lay down and rolled once or twice, and then fell to eating grass. When they were harnessed, they stepped sedately one behind the other over the sill of the barn door, sniffed the spring air, and waited patiently for the traces to be fastened. They were older than Almanzo, and he was going on ten.

They knew how to plow without stepping on corn, or making the furrows crooked. They knew how to harrow, and to turn at the end of the field. Almanzo would have enjoyed driving them more if they hadn't known so much.

He hitched them to the harrow. Last fall the fields had been plowed and covered with manure; now the lumpy soil must be harrowed.

Bess and Beauty stepped out willingly, not too fast, yet fast enough to harrow well. They liked to work in the springtime, after the long winter of standing in their stalls. Back and forth across the field they pulled the harrow, while Almanzo walked behind it, holding the reins. At the end of the row he turned the team around and set the harrow so that its teeth barely overlapped the strip already harrowed. Then he slapped the reins on the horses' rumps, shouted "Giddap!" and away they went again.

All over the countryside other boys were harrowing, too, turning up the moist earth to the sunshine. Far to the north the St. Lawrence River was a silver streak at the edge of the sky. The woods were clouds of delicate green. Birds hopped twittering on the stone fences, and squirrels frisked. Almanzo walked whistling behind his team.

When he harrowed the whole field across one way, then he harrowed it across the other way. The harrow's sharp teeth combed again and again through the earth, breaking up the lumps. All the soil must be made mellow and fine and smooth.

By and by Almanzo was too hungry to whistle. He grew hungrier and hungrier. It seemed that noon would never come. He wondered how many miles he'd walked. And still the sun seemed to stand still, the shadows seemed not to change at all. He was starving.

At last the sun stood overhead, the shadows were quite gone. Almanzo harrowed another row, and another. Then at last he heard the horns blowing, far and near.

Clear and joyful came the sound of Mother's big tin dinner-horn.

Bess and Beauty pricked up their ears and stepped more briskly. At the edge of the field toward the house they stopped. Almanzo unfastened the traces and looped them up, and leaving the harrow in the field, he climbed onto Beauty's broad back.

He rode down to the pumphouse and let the horses drink. He put them in their stall, took off their bridles, and gave them their grain. A good horseman always takes care of his horses before he eats or rests. But Almanzo hurried.

How good dinner was! And how he ate! Father heaped his plate again and again, and

Mother smiled and gave him two pieces of pie.

He felt better when he went back to work, but the afternoon seemed much longer than the morning. He was tired when he rode down to the barns at sunset, to do the chores. At supper he was drowsy, and as soon as he had eaten he climbed upstairs and went to bed. It was so good to stretch out on the soft bed. Before he could pull up the coverlet he fell fast asleep.

In just a minute Mother's candle-light shone on the stairs and she was calling. Another day had begun.

There was no time to lose, no time to waste in rest or play. The life of the earth comes up with a rush in the springtime. All the wild seeds of weed and thistle, the sprouts of vine and bush and tree, are trying to take the fields. Farmers must fight them with harrow and plow and hoe; they must plant the good seeds quickly.

Almanzo was a little soldier in this great battle. From dawn to dark he worked, from dark to dawn he slept, then he was up again and working.

He harrowed the potato field till the soil was smooth and mellow and every little sprouting weed was killed. Then he helped Royal take the seed potatoes from the bin in the cellar and cut them into pieces, leaving two or three eyes on each piece.

Potato plants have blossoms and seeds, but no one knows what kind of potato will grow from a potato seed. All the potatoes of one kind that have ever been grown have come from one potato. A potato is not a seed; it is part of a potato plant's root. Cut it up and plant it, and it will always make more potatoes just like itself.

Every potato has several little dents in it, that look like eyes. From these eyes the little roots grow down into the soil, and little leaves push up toward the sun. They eat up the piece of potato while they are small, before they are strong enough to take their food from the earth and the air.

Father was marking the field. The marker was a log with a row of wooden pegs driven into it, three and a half feet apart. One horse drew the log crosswise behind him, and the pegs made little furrows. Father marked the field lengthwise and crosswise, so the furrows made little squares. Then the planting began.

Father and Royal took their hoes, and Alice and Almanzo carried pails full of pieces of potato. Almanzo went in front of Royal and Alice went in front of Father, down the rows.

At the corner of each square, where the furrows crossed, Almanzo dropped one piece of potato. He must drop it exactly in the corner, so that the rows would be straight and could be plowed. Royal covered it with dirt and patted it firm with the hoe. Behind Alice, Father covered the pieces of potato that she dropped.

Planting potatoes was fun. A good smell came from the fresh earth and from the clover fields. Alice was pretty and gay, with the breeze blowing her curls and setting her hoopskirts swaying. Father was jolly, and they all talked while they worked.

Almanzo and Alice tried to drop the potatoes so fast that they'd have a minute at the end of a

126

row, to look for birds' nests or chase a lizard into the stone fence. But Father and Royal were never far behind. Father said:

"Hustle along there, son, hustle along!"

So they hustled, and when they were far enough ahead Almanzo plucked a grass-stem and made it whistle between his thumbs. Alice tried, but she could not do that. She could pucker her mouth and whistle. Royal teased her.

> "Whistling girls and crowing hens
> Always come to some bad ends."

Back and forth across the field they went, all morning, all afternoon, for three days. Then the potatoes were planted.

Then Father sowed the grain. He sowed a field of wheat for white bread, a field of rye for rye'n'injun bread, and a field of oats mixed with Canada peas, to feed the horses and cows next winter.

While Father sowed the grain, Almanzo followed him over the fields with Bess and Beauty, harrowing the seeds into the earth. Almanzo could not sow grain yet; he must practice a long

127

time before he could spread the seeds evenly. That is hard to do.

The heavy sack of grain hung from a strap over Father's left shoulder. As he walked, he took handfuls of grain from the sack. With a sweep of his arm and a bend of his wrist he let the little grains fly from his fingers. The sweep of his arm kept time with his steps, and when Father finished sowing a field every inch of ground had its evenly scattered seeds, nowhere too many or too few.

The seeds were too small to be seen on the ground, and you could not know how skillful a sower a man was, till the seeds came up. Father told Almanzo about a lazy, worthless boy who had been sent to sow a field. This boy did not want to work, so he poured the seeds out of his sack and went swimming. Nobody saw him. Afterward he harrowed the field, and no one knew what he had done. But the seeds knew, and the earth knew, and when even the boy had forgotten his wickedness, they told it. Weeds took that field.

When all the grain was sowed, Almanzo and Alice planted the carrots. They had sacks full of the little, red, round carrot seeds hanging from their shoulders, like Father's big seed-sack. Father had marked the carrot field lengthwise, with a marker whose teeth were only eighteen inches apart. Almanzo and Alice, with the carrot seeds, went up and down the long field, straddling the little furrows.

Now the weather was so warm that they could go barefooted. Their bare feet felt good in the air and the soft dirt. They dribbled the carrot seeds into the furrows, and with their feet they pushed the dirt over the seeds and pressed it down.

Almanzo could see his feet, but of course Alice's were hidden under her skirts. Her hoops rounded out, and she had to pull them back and stoop to drop the seeds neatly into the furrow.

Almanzo asked her if she didn't want to be a boy. She said yes, she did. Then she said no, she didn't.

"Boys aren't pretty like girls, and they can't wear ribbons."

"I don't care how pretty I be," Almanzo said. "And I wouldn't wear ribbons anyhow."

"Well, I like to make butter and I like to patch quilts. And cook, and sew, and spin. Boys can't do that. But even if I be a girl, I can drop potatoes and sow carrots and drive horses as well as you can."

"You can't whistle on a grass stem," Almanzo said.

At the end of the row he looked at the ash

tree's crumpled new leaves, and asked Alice if she knew when to plant corn. She didn't, so he told her. Corn-planting time is when the ash leaves are as big as squirrels' ears.

"How big a squirrel?" Alice asked.

"Just an ordinary squirrel."

"Well, those leaves are as big as a baby squirrel's ears. And it isn't corn-planting time."

For a minute Almanzo didn't know what to think. Then he said:

"A baby squirrel isn't a squirrel; it's a kitten."

"But it's just as much a squirrel——"

"No it isn't. It's a kitten. Little cats are kittens, and little foxes are kittens, and little squirrels are kittens. A kitten isn't a cat, and a kitten isn't a squirrel, either."

"Oh," Alice said.

When the ash leaves were big enough, Almanzo helped to plant corn. The field had been marked with the potato marker, and Father and Royal and Almanzo planted it together.

They wore bags of seed corn tied around their waists like aprons, and they carried hoes. At the

131

corner of each square, where the furrows crossed, they stirred up the soil with the hoe, and made a shallow hollow in it, dropped two grains of corn into the hollow, and covered them with dirt and patted the dirt firm.

Father and Royal worked fast. Their hands and their hoes made exactly the same movements every time. Three quick slashes and a dab with the hoe, a flash of the hand, then a scoop and two pats with the hoe, and that hill of corn was planted. Then they made one quick stride forward, and did it again.

But Almanzo had never planted corn before. He did not handle the hoe so well. He had to trot two steps where Royal or Father took one, because his legs were shorter. Father and Royal were ahead of him all the time; he could not keep up. One of them finished out his row each time, so that he could start even again. He did not like that. But he knew he would plant corn as fast as anybody, when his legs were longer.

Chapter 12

Tin-Peddler

ONE evening after sunset Almanzo saw a white horse pulling a large, bright-red cart up the road, and he yelled,

"The tin-peddler's coming! The tin-peddler's coming!"

Alice ran out of the henhouse with her apron full of eggs. Mother and Eliza Jane came to the kitchen door. Royal popped out of the pumphouse. And the young horses put their heads through the windows of their stalls and whinnied to the big white horse.

Nick Brown, the tin-peddler, was a jolly, fat man, who told stories and sang songs. In the springtime he went driving along all the country roads, bringing news from far and near.

His cart was like a little house, swinging on stout leather straps between four high wheels. It had a door on either side, and from its rear a platform slanted upward like a bird's tail, held in place by straps that went to the cart's top. There was a fancy railing all around the top of the cart, and the cart and the platform and the wheels were all painted bright red, with beautiful scrolls painted bright yellow. High in front rode Nick Brown, on a red seat above the rump of the sturdy white horse.

Almanzo and Alice and Royal and even Eliza Jane were waiting when the cart stopped by the kitchen porch, and Mother was smiling in the doorway.

"How do you do, Mr. Brown!" she called.

"Put up your horse and come right in, supper's almost ready!" And Father called from the barn, "Drive into the Buggy-house, Nick, there's plenty of room!"

Almanzo unhitched the sleek, big horse and led him to water, then put him in a stall and gave him a double feed of oats and plenty of hay. Mr. Brown carefully currycombed and brushed him, and rubbed him down with clean cloths. He was a good horseman. After that he looked at all the stock and gave his opinion of it. He admired Star and Bright and praised Father's colts.

"You ought to get a good price for those coming four-year-olds," he said to Father. "Over by Saranac, the New York buyers are looking for driving-horses. One of them paid two hundred dollars apiece last week for a team not a mite better than these."

Almanzo could not speak while grown-ups were talking, of course. But he could listen. He didn't miss anything that Mr. Brown said. And he knew that the best time of all was coming after supper.

Nick Brown could tell more funny stories and sing more songs than any other man. He said so himself, and it was true.

"Yes, sir," he said, "I'll back myself, not alone against any man, but against any crowd of men. I'll tell story for story and sing song for song, as long as you'll bring men up against me, and when they're all done, I'll tell the last story and sing the last song."

Father knew this was true. He had heard Nick Brown do it, in Mr. Case's store in Malone.

So after supper they all settled down by the heater, and Mr. Brown began. It was after nine o'clock before anyone went to bed, and Almanzo's sides ached with laughing.

Next morning after breakfast Mr. Brown hitched the white horse to the cart and drove it up to the kitchen porch, and he opened the red doors.

Inside that cart was everything ever made of tin. On shelves along the walls were nests of bright tin pails, and pans, and basins, cake-pans, pie-pans, bread-pans and dishpans. Overhead

dangled cups and dippers, skimmers and strainers, steamers, colanders, and graters. There were tin horns, tin whistles, toy tin dishes and pattypans, there were all kinds of little animals made of tin and brightly painted.

Mr. Brown had made all these himself, in the winter-time, and every piece was made of good

137

thick tin, well made and solidly soldered.

Mother brought the big rag-bags from the attic, and emptied on the porch floor all the rags she had saved during the last year. Mr. Brown examined the good, clean rags of wool and linen, while Mother looked at the shining tinware, and they began to trade.

For a long time they talked and argued. Shining tinware and piles of rags were all over the porch. For every pile of rags that Nick Brown added to the big pile, Mother asked more tinware than he wanted to trade her. They were both having a good time, joking and laughing and trading. At last Mr. Brown said,

"Well, ma'am, I'll trade you the milk-pans and pails, the colander and skimmer, and the three baking-pans, but not the dishpan, and that's my last offer."

"Very well, Mr. Brown," Mother said, unexpectedly. She had got exactly what she wanted. Almanzo knew she did not need the dishpan; she had set it out only to bargain with. Mr. Brown knew that, too, now. He looked surprised, and he looked respectfully at Mother. Mother was a good, shrewd trader. She had bested Mr. Brown. But he was satisfied, too, because he had got plenty of good rags for his tinware.

He gathered up the rags and tied them into a bale, and heaved the bale onto the slanting platform behind his cart. The platform and the railing around the top of the cart were made to hold the rags he took in trade.

Then Mr. Brown rubbed his hands together and looked around, smiling.

"Well now," he said, "I wonder what these young folks would like!"

He gave Eliza Jane six little diamond-shaped patty-pans to bake little cakes in, and he gave Alice six heart-shaped ones, and he gave Almanzo a tin horn painted red. They all said:

"Thank you, Mr. Brown!"

Then Mr. Brown climbed to his high seat and took up the reins. The big white horse stepped out eagerly, well fed and brushed and rested. The red cart went past the house and lurched

139

into the road, and Mr. Brown began to whistle.

Mother had her tinware for that year, and Almanzo had his loud-squawking horn, and Nick Brown rode whistling away between the green trees and the fields. Until he came again next spring they would remember his news and laugh at his jokes, and behind the horses in the fields Almanzo would whistle the songs he had sung.

Chapter 13

The Strange Dog

NICK BROWN had said that New York horse-buyers were in the neighborhood, so every night Father gave the four-year-old colts a special, careful grooming. The four-year-olds were already perfectly broken, and Almanzo wanted so much to help groom them that Father let him. But he was allowed to go into their stalls only when Father was there.

Carefully Almanzo currycombed and brushed their shining brown sides, and their smooth round haunches and slender legs. Then he rubbed them down with clean cloths. He combed and braided their black manes and their long black tails. With a little brush he oiled their curved hoofs, till they shone black as Mother's polished stove.

He was careful never to move suddenly and startle them. He talked to them while he worked, in a gentle, low voice. The colts nibbled his sleeve with their lips, and nuzzled at his pockets for the apples he brought them. They arched their necks when he rubbed their velvety noses, and their soft eyes shone.

Almanzo knew that in the whole world there was nothing so beautiful, so fascinating, as beautiful horses. When he thought that it would be years and years before he could have a little colt to teach and take care of, he could hardly bear it.

One evening the horse-buyer came riding into the barnyard. He was a strange horse-buyer; Father had never seen him before. He was dressed in city clothes, of machine-made cloth, and he tapped his shining tall boots with a little red whip. His black eyes were close to his thin nose; his black beard was trimmed into a point, and the ends of his mustache were waxed and twisted.

He looked very strange, standing in the barn-yard and thoughtfully twisting one end of his mustache into a sharper point.

Father led out the colts. They were perfectly matched Morgans, exactly the same size, the same shape, the same bright brown all over, with the same white stars on their foreheads. They arched their necks and picked up their little feet daintily.

"Four years old in May, sound in wind and limb, not a blemish on them," Father said. "Broken to drive double or single. They're high-spirited, full of ginger, and gentle as kittens. A lady can drive them."

Almanzo listened. He was excited, but he re-membered carefully everything that Father and the horse-buyer said. Some day he would be trading horses, himself.

The buyer felt the colts' legs, he opened their mouths and looked at their teeth. Father had nothing to fear from that; he had told the truth about the colts' age. Then the buyer stood back and watched, while Father took each colt on a long rope and made it walk, trot, and gallop in a circle around him.

"Look at that action," Father said.

The shining black manes and tails rippled in the air. Brown lights flowed over their smooth bodies, and their delicate feet seemed hardly to touch the ground. Round and round they went, like a tune.

The buyer looked. He tried to find fault, but he couldn't. The colts stood still, and Father waited. Finally the buyer offered $175 apiece.

Father said he couldn't take less than $225. Almanzo knew he said that, because he wanted $200. Nick Brown had told him that horse-buyers were paying that much.

Then Father hitched both colts to the buggy. He and the buyer climbed in, and away they went down the road. The colts' heads were high, their noses stretched out; their manes and tails blew in the wind of their speed, and their flashing legs moved all together, as though the colts were one colt. The buggy was gone out of sight in a moment.

Almanzo knew he must go on with the chores. He went into the barn and took the pitchfork; then he put it down and came out to watch for the colts' return.

When they came back, Father and the buyer had not agreed on the price. Father tugged at his beard, and the buyer twisted his mustache. The buyer talked about the expense of taking the colts to New York, and about the low prices there. He had to think of his profit. The best he could offer was $175.

Father said: "I'll split the difference. Two hundred dollars, and that's my last price."

The buyer thought, and answered, "I don't see my way clear to pay that."

"All right," Father said. "No hard feelings, and we'll be glad to have you stay to supper."

He began to unhitch the colts. The buyer said:

145

"Over by Saranac they're selling better horses than these for one hundred and seventy-five dollars."

Father didn't answer. He unhitched the colts and led them toward their stalls. Then the buyer said:

"All right, two hundred it is. I'll lose money by it, but here you are." He took a fat wallet out of his pocket and gave Father $200 to bind the bargain. "Bring them to town tomorrow, and get the rest."

The colts were sold, at Father's price.

The buyer would not stay to supper. He rode away, and Father took the money to Mother in the kitchen. Mother exclaimed:

"You mean to say we must keep all that money in the house overnight!"

"It's too late to take it to the bank," Father said. "We're safe enough. Nobody but us knows the money's here."

"I declare I sha'n't sleep a wink!"

"The Lord will take care of us," Father said.

"The Lord helps them that help themselves,"

146

Mother replied. "I wish to goodness that money was safe in the bank."

It was already past chore-time, and Almanzo had to hurry to the barn with the milk-pails. If cows are not milked at exactly the same time, night and morning, they will not give so much milk. Then there were the mangers and stalls to clean and all the stock to feed. It was almost eight o'clock before everything was done, and Mother was keeping supper warm.

Supper-time was not as cheerful as usual. There was a dark, heavy feeling about that money. Mother had hidden it in the pantry, then she hid it in the linen-closet. After supper she began setting the sponge for tomorrow's baking, and worrying again about the money. Her hands flew, the bread sponge made little plopping sounds under her spoon, and she was saying:

"It don't seem as though anybody'd think to look between sheets in the closet, but I declare I— *What's that!*"

They all jumped. They held their breaths and listened.

"*Something or somebody's prowling round this house!*" Mother breathed.

All you could see when you looked at the windows was blackness outside.

"Pshaw! 'Twa'n't anything," Father said.

"I tell you I heard something!"

"I didn't," Father said.

"Royal," said Mother, "you go look."

Royal opened the kitchen door and peered into the dark. After a minute he said,

"It's nothing but a stray dog."

"Drive it away!" said Mother. Royal went out and drove it away.

Almanzo wished he had a dog. But a little dog digs up the garden and chases hens and sucks eggs, and a big dog may kill sheep. Mother always said there was stock enough on the place, without a dirty dog.

She set away the bread sponge. Almanzo washed his feet. He had to wash his feet every night, when he went barefoot. He was washing them when they all heard a stealthy sound on the back porch.

Mother's eyes were big. Royal said:

"It's only that dog."

He opened the door. At first they saw nothing, and Mother's eyes got bigger. Then they saw a big, thin dog cringing away in the shadows. His ribs showed under his fur.

"Oh, Mother, the poor dog!" Alice cried.

"Please, Mother, can't I give him just a little bit to eat?"

"Goodness, child, yes!" Mother said. "You can drive him away in the morning, Royal."

Alice set out a pan of food for the dog. He dared not come near it while the door was open, but when Almanzo shut the door they heard him chewing. Mother tried the door twice to make sure it was locked.

The dark came into the kitchen when they left it with the candles, and the dark looked in through the dining-room windows. Mother locked both dining-room doors, and she even went into the parlor and tried the parlor door, though it was always kept locked.

Almanzo lay in bed a long time, listening and staring at the dark. But at last he fell asleep, and he did not know what happened in the night till Mother told it next morning.

She had put the money under Father's socks in the bureau drawer. But after she went to bed, she got up again and put it under her pillow. She did not think she would sleep at all, but she must have, because in the night something woke her. She sat bolt upright in bed. Father was sound asleep.

The moon was shining and she could see the lilac bush in the yard. Everything was still. The clock struck eleven. Then Mother's blood ran cold; she heard a low, savage growl.

She got out of bed and went to the window. The strange dog stood under it, bristling and showing his teeth. He acted as though somebody was in the woodlot.

Mother stood listening and looking. It was dark under the trees, and she could not see any-one. But the dog growled savagely at the dark-ness.

Mother watched. She heard the clock strike midnight, and after a long time it struck one o'clock. The dog walked up and down by the picket fence, growling. At last he lay down, but he kept his head up and his ears pricked, listen-ing. Mother went softly back to bed.

At dawn the dog was gone. They looked for him, but they could not find him anywhere.

But his tracks were in the yard, and on the other side of the fence, in the woodlot, Father found the tracks of two men's boots.

He hitched up at once, before breakfast, and tied the colts behind the buggy and drove to Malone. He put the $200 in the bank. He delivered the colts to the horse-buyer and got the other $200, and put that in the bank, too.

When he came back he told Mother.

"You were right. We came near being robbed last night."

A farmer near Malone had sold a team the week before, and kept the money in his house. That night robbers broke into his room while he was asleep. They tied up his wife and children, and they beat him almost to death, to make him tell where the money was hidden. They took the money and got away. The sheriff was looking for them.

"I wouldn't be surprised if that horse-buyer had a hand in it," Father said. "Who else knew we had money in the house? But it couldn't be

152

proved. I made inquiry, and he was at the hotel in Malone last night."

Mother said she would always believe that Providence had sent the strange dog to watch over them. Almanzo thought perhaps he stayed because Alice fed him.

"Maybe he was sent to try us," Mother said. "Maybe the Lord was merciful to us because we were merciful to him."

They never saw the strange dog again. Perhaps he was a poor lost dog and the food that Alice gave him made him strong enough to find his way home again.

Chapter 14

Sheep-Shearing

NOW the meadows and pastures were velvety with thick grass, and the weather was warm. It was time to shear sheep.

On a sunny morning Pierre and Louis went with Almanzo into the pasture and they drove the sheep down to the washing-pens. The long pen ran from the grassy pasture into the clear, deep water of Trout River. It had two gates opening into the pasture, and between the gates a short fence ran to the water's edge.

Pierre and Louis kept the flock from running

away, while Almanzo took hold of a woolly sheep and pushed it through one gate. In the pen Father and Lazy John caught hold of it. Then Almanzo pushed another one through, and Royal and French Joe caught it. The other sheep stared and bleated, and the two sheep struggled and kicked and yelled. But the men rubbed their wool full of brown soft-soap and dragged them into the deep water.

There the sheep had to swim. The men stood waist-deep in the swift water, and held onto the sheep and scrubbed them well. All the dirt came out of their wool and floated downstream with the soap suds.

When the other sheep saw this, every one of them cried, "Baa-aa-aa, baa-aa-aa!" and they all tried to run away. But Almanzo and Pierre and Louis ran yelling around the flock, and brought it back again to the gate.

As soon as a sheep was clean, the men made it swim around the end of the dividing fence, and they boosted it up the bank into the outer side of the pen. The poor sheep came out bleating and dripping wet, but the sun soon dried it fluffy and white.

As fast as the men let go of one sheep, Almanzo pushed another into the pen, and they caught it and soaped it and dragged it into the river.

Washing sheep was fun for everybody but the sheep. The men splashed and shouted and laughed in the water, and the boys ran and shouted in the pasture. The sun was warm on their backs and the grass was cool under bare feet, and all their laughter was small in the wide, pleasant stillness of the green fields and meadows.

One sheep butted John; he sat down in the river and the water went over his head. Joe shouted,

"Now if you had soap in your wool, John, you'd be ready for shearing!"

When evening came, all the sheep were washed. Clean and fluffy-white, they scattered up the slope, nibbling the grass, and the pasture looked like a snowball bush in bloom.

156

Next morning John came before breakfast, and Father hurried Almanzo from the table. He took a wedge of apple pie and went out to the pasture, smelling the clover and eating the spicy apples and flaky crust in big mouthfuls. He licked his fingers, and then he rounded up the sheep and drove them across the dewy grass, into the sheepfold in the South Barn.

Father had cleaned the sheepfold and built a platform across one end of it. He and Lazy John each caught a sheep, set it up on the platform, and began cutting off its wool with long shears. The thick white mat of wool peeled back, all in one piece, and the sheep was left in bare pink skin.

With the last snick of the shears the whole fleece fell on the platform, and the naked sheep jumped off it, yelling, "Baa-aa-aa!" All the other sheep yelled back at the sight, but already Father and John were shearing two more.

Royal rolled the fleece tightly and tied it with twine, and Almanzo carried it upstairs and laid

157

it on the loft floor. He ran upstairs and down again as fast as he could, but another fleece was always ready for him.

Father and Lazy John were good sheep-shearers. Their long shears snipped through the thick wool like lightning; they cut close to the sheep, but never cut its pink skin. This was a hard thing to do, because Father's sheep were prize Merinos. Merinos have the finest wool, but their skin lies in deep wrinkles, and it is hard to get all the wool without cutting them.

Almanzo was working fast, running upstairs with the fleeces. They were so heavy that he could carry only one at a time. He didn't mean to idle, but when he saw the tabby barn-cat hurrying past with a mouse, he knew she was taking it to her new kittens.

He ran after her, and far up under the eaves of the Big Barn he found the little nest in the hay, with four kittens in it. The tabby cat curled herself around them, loudly purring, and the black slits in her eyes widened and narrowed and

158

widened again. The kittens' tiny pink mouths uttered tiny meows, their naked little paws had wee white claws, and their eyes were shut.

When Almanzo came back to the sheepfold,

six fleeces were waiting, and Father spoke to him sternly.

"Son," he said, "see to it you keep up with us after this."

"Yes, Father," Almanzo answered, hurrying. But he heard Lazy John say:

"He can't do it. We'll be through before he is."

Then Father laughed and said:

"That's so, John. He can't keep up with us."

Almanzo made up his mind that he'd show them. If he hurried fast enough, he could keep up. Before noon he had caught up with Royal, and had to wait while a fleece was tied. So he said:

"You see I can keep up with you!"

"Oh no, you can't!" said John. "We'll beat you. We'll be through before you are. Wait and see."

Then they all laughed at Almanzo.

They were laughing when they heard the dinner horn. Father and John finished the sheep they were shearing, and went to the house.

Royal tied the last fleece and left it, and Almanzo still had to carry it upstairs. Now he understood what they meant. But he thought:

"I won't let them beat me."

He found a short rope and tied it around the neck of a sheep that wasn't sheared. He led the sheep to the stairs, and then step by step he tugged and boosted her upward. She bleated all the way, but he got her into the loft. He tied her near the fleeces and gave her some hay to keep her quiet. Then he went to dinner.

All that afternoon Lazy John and Royal kept telling him to hurry or they'd beat him. Almanzo answered:

"No, you won't. I can keep up with you."

Then they laughed at him.

He snatched up every fleece as soon as Royal tied it, and hurried upstairs and ran down again. They laughed to see him hurrying, and they kept saying:

"Oh no, you won't beat us! We'll be through first!"

Just before chore-time, Father and John raced

to shear the last two sheep. Father beat. Almanzo ran with the fleece, and was back before the last one was ready. Royal tied it, and then he said:

"We're all through! Almanzo, we beat you! We beat you!" Royal and John burst into a great roar of laughter, and even Father laughed.

Then Almanzo said:

"No, you haven't beat me. I've got a fleece upstairs that you haven't sheared yet."

They stopped laughing, surprised. At that very minute the sheep in the loft, hearing all the other sheep let out to pasture, cried, "Baa-aa-aa!"

Almanzo shouted: "There's the fleece! I've got it upstairs and you haven't sheared it! I beat you! I beat you!"

John and Royal looked so funny that he couldn't stop laughing. Father roared with laughter.

"The joke's on you, John!" Father shouted. "He laughs best who laughs last!"

Chapter 15

Cold Snap

THAT was a cold, late spring. The dawns were chilly, and at noon the sunlight was cool. The trees unfolded their leaves slowly; the peas and beans, the carrots and corn, stood waiting for warmth and did not grow.

When the rush of spring's work was over, Almanzo had to go to school again. Only small children went to the spring term of school, and he wished he were old enough to stay home. He didn't like to sit and study a book when there were so many interesting things to do.

Father hauled the fleeces to the carding-machine in Malone, and brought home the soft, long rolls of wool, combed out straight and fine. Mother didn't card her own wool any more, since there was a machine that did it on shares. But she dyed it.

Alice and Eliza Jane were gathering roots and barks in the woods, and Royal was building huge bonfires in the yard. They boiled the roots and the bark in big caldrons over the fires, and they dipped the long skeins of wool thread that Mother had spun, and lifted them out on sticks, all colored brown and red and blue. When Almanzo went home from school the clothes-lines were hanging full of the colored skeins.

Mother was making soft-soap, too. All the winter's ashes had been saved in a barrel; now water was poured over them, and lye was dripping out of the little hole in the bottom of the barrel. Mother measured the lye into a caldron, and added pork rinds and all the waste pork fat and beef fat that she had been saving all winter.

164

The caldron boiled, and the lye and the fat made soap.

Almanzo could have kept the bonfires burning, he could have dipped the brown, slimy soap out of the caldron and filled the tubs with it. But he had to go to school.

He watched the moon anxiously, for in the dark of the moon in May he could stay out of school and plant pumpkins.

Then in the chill, early morning he tied a pouch full of pumpkin seeds around his waist and went to the cornfield. All the dark field had a thin green veil of weeds over it now. The small blades of corn were not growing well because of the cold.

At every second hill of corn, in every second row, Almanzo knelt down and took a thin, flat pumpkin-seed between his thumb and finger. He pushed the seed, sharp point down, into the ground.

It was chill work at first, but pretty soon the sun was higher. The air and the earth smelled good, and it was fun to poke his finger and thumb into the soft soil and leave the seed there to grow.

Day after day he worked, till all the pumpkins were planted, and then he begged to hoe and thin the carrots. He hoed all the weeds away from the long rows, and he pulled the little feathery carrot-tops, till those that were left stood two inches apart.

He didn't hurry at all. No one had ever taken such pains with carrots as he did, because he didn't want to go back to school. He made the work last till there were only three more days of school; then the spring term ended and he could work all summer.

First he helped hoe the cornfield. Father plowed between the rows, and Royal and Almanzo with hoes killed every weed that was left, and hoed around each hill of corn. Slash, slash went the hoes all day, stirring the earth around the young shoots of corn and the first two flat leaves of the pumpkins.

Two acres of corn Almanzo hoed, and then he hoed two acres of potatoes. That finished

166

the hoeing for awhile, and now it was straw-berry-time.

Wild strawberries were few that year, and late, because frost had killed the first blossoms. Almanzo had to go far through the woods to fill his pail full of the small, sweet, fragrant berries.

When he found them clustered under their green leaves, he couldn't help eating some. He snipped off the green twigs of wintergreen and ate them, too. And he nibbled with his teeth the sweet-sour woodsorrel's stems, right up to their frail lavender blossoms. He stopped to shy stones at the frisking squirrels, and he left his pail on the banks of streams and went wading, chasing the minnows. But he never came home till his pail was full.

Then there were strawberries and cream for supper, and next day Mother would make straw-berry preserves.

"I never saw corn grow so slowly," Father worried. He plowed the field again, and again Almanzo helped Royal to hoe the corn. But the little shoots stood still. On the first of July they

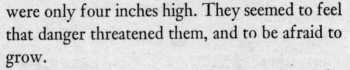

were only four inches high. They seemed to feel that danger threatened them, and to be afraid to grow.

It was three days to Independence Day, the fourth day of July. Then it was two days. Then it was one day, and that night Almanzo had to take a bath, though it wasn't Saturday. Next morning they were all going to the celebration

168

in Malone. Almanzo could hardly wait till morning. There would be a band, and speeches, and the brass cannon would be fired.

The air was still and cold that night, and the stars had a wintry look. After supper Father went to the barns again. He shut the doors and the little wooden windows of the horses' stalls, and he put the ewes with lambs into the fold.

When he came in, Mother asked if it was any warmer. Father shook his head.

"I do believe it is going to freeze," he said.

"Pshaw! surely not!" Mother replied. But she looked worried.

Sometime in the night Almanzo felt cold, but he was too sleepy to do anything about it. Then he heard Mother calling:

"Royal! Almanzo!" He was too sleepy to open his eyes.

"Boys, get up! Hurry!" Mother called. "The corn's frozen!"

He tumbled out of bed and pulled on his trousers. He couldn't keep his eyes open, his hands were clumsy, and big yawns almost dislocated his jaw. He staggered downstairs behind Royal.

Mother and Eliza Jane and Alice were putting on their hoods and shawls. The kitchen was cold; the fire had not been lighted. Outdoors everything looked strange. The grass was white with frost, and a cold green streak was in the eastern sky, but the air was dark.

Father hitched Bess and Beauty to the wagon. Royal pumped the watering-trough full. Almanzo helped Mother and the girls bring tubs and pails, and Father set barrels in the wagon. They filled the tubs and barrels full of water, and then they walked behind the wagon to the cornfield.

All the corn was frozen. The little leaves were stiff, and broke if you touched them. Only cold water would save the life of the corn. Every hill must be watered before the sunshine touched it, or the little plants would die. There would be no corn-crop that year.

The wagon stopped at the edge of the field. Father and Mother and Royal and Eliza Jane and Alice and Almanzo filled their pails with water, and they all went to work, as fast as they could.

Almanzo tried to hurry, but the pail was heavy and his legs were short. His wet fingers were cold, the water slopped against his legs, and he was terribly sleepy. He stumbled along the rows, and at every hill of corn he poured a little water over the frozen leaves.

The field seemed enormous. There were thousands and thousands of hills of corn. Almanzo began to be hungry. But he couldn't stop to complain. He must hurry, hurry, hurry, to save the corn.

The green in the east turned pink. Every moment the light brightened. At first the dark had been like a mist over the endless field, now Almanzo could see to the end of the long rows. He tried to work faster.

In an instant the earth turned from black to gray. The sun was coming to kill the corn.

Almanzo ran to fill his pail; he ran back. He ran down the rows, splashing water on the hills of corn. His shoulders ached and his arm ached and there was a pain in his side. The soft earth hung on to his feet. He was terribly hungry. But every splash of water saved a hill of corn.

In the gray light the corn had faint shadows now. All at once pale sunshine came over the field.

"Keep on!" Father shouted. So they all kept on; they didn't stop.

But in a little while Father gave up. "No use!" he called. Nothing would save the corn after the sunshine touched it.

Almanzo set down his pail and straightened up against the ache in his back. He stood and looked at the cornfield. All the others stood and looked, too, and did not say anything. They had watered almost three acres. A quarter of an acre had not been watered. It was lost.

Almanzo trudged back to the wagon and climbed in. Father said:

"Let's be thankful we saved most of it."

They rode sleepily down to the barns. Almanzo was not quite awake yet, and he was tired and cold and hungry. His hands were clumsy, doing the chores. But most of the corn was saved.

Chapter 16

Independence Day

ALMANZO was eating breakfast before he remembered that this was the Fourth of July. He felt more cheerful.

It was like Sunday morning. After breakfast he scrubbed his face with soft soap till it shone, and he parted his wet hair and combed it sleekly down. He put on his sheep's-gray trousers and his shirt of French calico, and his vest and his short round coat.

Mother had made his new suit in the new style. The coat fastened at the throat with a little flap of cloth, then the two sides slanted back to show his vest, and they rounded off over his trousers' pockets.

He put on his round straw hat, which Mother had made of braided oat-straws, and he was all dressed up for Independence Day. He felt very fine.

Father's shining horses were hitched to the shining, red-wheeled buggy, and they all drove away in the cool sunshine. All the country had a holiday air. Nobody was working in the fields, and along the road the people in their Sunday clothes were driving to town.

Father's swift horses passed them all. They passed by wagons and carts and buggies. They passed gray horses and black horses and dappled-gray horses. Almanzo waved his hat whenever he sailed past anyone he knew, and he would have been perfectly happy if only he had been driving that swift, beautiful team.

At the church sheds in Malone he helped Father unhitch. Mother and the girls and Royal hurried away. But Almanzo would rather help with the horses than do anything else. He couldn't drive them, but he could tie their halters and buckle on their blankets, and stroke their soft noses and give them hay.

Then he went out with Father and they walked on the crowded sidewalks. All the stores were closed, but ladies and gentlemen were walking up and down and talking. Ruffled little girls carried parasols, and all the boys were dressed up, like Almanzo. Flags were everywhere, and in the Square the band was playing "Yankee Doodle." The fifes tooted and the flutes shrilled and the drums came in with rub-a-dub-dub.

> "Yankee Doodle went to town,
>   Riding on a pony,
>   He stuck a feather in his hat,
>   And called it macaroni!"

Even grown-ups had to keep time to it. And there, in the corner of the Square, were the two brass cannons!

The Square was not really square. The railroad made it three-cornered. But everybody called it the Square, anyway. It was fenced, and grass grew there. Benches stood in rows on the grass, and people were filing between the benches and sitting down as they did in church.

Almanzo went with Father to one of the best front seats. All the important men stopped to

shake hands with Father. The crowd kept coming till all the seats were full, and still there were people outside the fence.

The band stopped playing, and the minister prayed. Then the band tuned up again and

everybody rose. Men and boys took off their hats. The band played, and everybody sang.

"Oh, say, can you see by the dawn's early light,
What so proudly we hailed at the twilight's last gleaming,
Whose broad stripes and bright stars through the perilous night,
O'er the ramparts we watched were so gallantly streaming?"

From the top of the flagpole, up against the blue sky, the Stars and Stripes were fluttering. Everybody looked at the American flag, and Almanzo sang with all his might.

Then everyone sat down, and a Congressman stood up on the platform. Slowly and solemnly he read the Declaration of Independence.

"When in the course of human events it becomes necessary for one people . . . to assume among the powers of the earth the separate and equal station. . . . We hold these truths to be self-evident, that all men are created equal. . . ."

Almanzo felt solemn and very proud.

Then two men made long political speeches.

One believed in high tariffs, and one believed in free trade. All the grown-ups listened hard, but Almanzo did not understand the speeches very well and he began to be hungry. He was glad when the band played again.

The music was so gay; the bandsmen in their blue and red and their brass buttons tootled merrily, and the fat drummer beat rat-a-tat-tat on the drum. All the flags were fluttering and everybody was happy, because they were free and independent and this was Independence Day. And it was time to eat dinner.

Almanzo helped Father feed the horses while Mother and the girls spread the picnic lunch on the grass in the churchyard. Many others were picnicking there, too, and after he had eaten all he could Almanzo went back to the Square.

There was a lemonade-stand by the hitching-posts. A man sold pink lemonade, a nickel a glass, and a crowd of the town boys were standing around him. Cousin Frank was there. Almanzo had a drink at the town pump, but Frank said he was going to buy lemonade. He had a nickel.

He walked up to the stand and bought a glass of the pink lemonade and drank it slowly. He smacked his lips and rubbed his stomach and said:

"Mmmm! Why don't you buy some?"

"Where'd you get the nickel?" Almanzo asked. He had never had a nickel. Father gave him a penny every Sunday to put in the collection-box in church; he had never had any other money.

"My father gave it to me," Frank bragged. "My father gives me a nickel every time I ask him."

"Well, so would my father if I asked him," said Almanzo.

"Well, why don't you ask him?" Frank did not believe that Father would give Almanzo a nickel. Almanzo did not know whether Father would, or not.

"Because I don't want to," he said.

"He wouldn't give you a nickel," Frank said.

"He would, too."

"I dare you to ask him," Frank said. The

other boys were listening. Almanzo put his hands in his pockets and said:

"I'd just as lief ask him if I wanted to."

"Yah, you're scared!" Frank jeered. "Double dare! Double dare!"

Father was a little way down the street, talking to Mr. Paddock, the wagon-maker. Almanzo walked slowly toward them. He was faint-hearted, but he had to go. The nearer he got to Father, the more he dreaded asking for a nickel. He had never before thought of doing such a thing. He was sure Father would not give it to him.

He waited till Father stopped talking and looked at him.

"What is it, son?" Father asked.

Almanzo was scared. "Father," he said.

"Well, son?"

"Father," Almanzo said, "would you—would you give me—a nickel?"

He stood there while Father and Mr. Paddock looked at him, and he wished he could get away. Finally Father asked:

"What for?"

Almanzo looked down at his moccasins and muttered:

"Frank had a nickel. He bought pink lemonade."

"Well," Father said, slowly, "if Frank treated you, it's only right you should treat him." Father put his hand in his pocket. Then he stopped and asked:

"Did Frank treat you to lemonade?"

Almanzo wanted so badly to get the nickel that he nodded. Then he squirmed and said:

"No, Father."

Father looked at him a long time. Then he took out his wallet and opened it, and slowly he took out a round, big silver half-dollar. He asked:

"Almanzo, do you know what this is?"

"Half a dollar," Almanzo answered.

"Yes. But do you know what half a dollar is?"

Almanzo didn't know it was anything but half a dollar.

"It's work, son," Father said. "That's what money is; it's hard work."

Mr. Paddock chuckled. "The boy's too young, Wilder," he said. "You can't make a youngster understand that."

"Almanzo's smarter than you think," said Father.

Almanzo didn't understand at all. He wished he could get away. But Mr. Paddock was looking at Father just as Frank looked at Almanzo when he double-dared him, and Father had said Almanzo was smart, so Almanzo tried to look like a smart boy. Father asked:

"You know how to raise potatoes, Almanzo?"

"Yes," Almanzo said.

"Say you have a seed potato in the spring, what do you do with it?"

"You cut it up," Almanzo said.

"Go on, son."

"Then you harrow—first you manure the field, and plow it. Then you harrow, and mark the ground. And plant the potatoes, and plow them, and hoe them. You plow and hoe them twice."

"That's right, son. And then?"

"Then you dig them and put them down cellar."

"Yes. Then you pick them over all winter; you throw out all the little ones and the rotten ones. Come spring, you load them up and haul them here to Malone, and you sell them. And if you get a good price, son, how much do you get to show for all that work? How much do you get for half a bushel of potatoes?"

"Half a dollar," Almanzo said.

"Yes," said Father. "That's what's in this half-dollar, Almanzo. The work that raised half a bushel of potatoes is in it."

Almanzo looked at the round piece of money that Father held up. It looked small, compared with all that work.

"You can have it, Almanzo," Father said. Almanzo could hardly believe his ears. Father gave him the heavy half-dollar.

"It's yours," said Father. "You could buy a sucking pig with it, if you want to. You could raise it, and it would raise a litter of pigs, worth four, five dollars apiece. Or you can trade that

184

half-dollar for lemonade, and drink it up. You do as you want, it's your money."

Almanzo forgot to say thank you. He held the half-dollar a minute, then he put his hand in his pocket and went back to the boys by the lemonade-stand. The man was calling out,

"Step this way, step this way! Ice-cold lemonade, pink lemonade, only five cents a glass! Only half a dime, ice-cold pink lemonade! The twentieth part of a dollar!"

Frank asked Almanzo:

"Where's the nickel?"

"He didn't give me a nickel," said Almanzo, and Frank yelled:

"Yah, yah! I told you he wouldn't! I told you so!"

"He gave me half a dollar," said Almanzo.

The boys wouldn't believe it till he showed them. Then they crowded around, waiting for him to spend it. He showed it to them all, and put it back in his pocket.

"I'm going to look around," he said, "and buy me a good little sucking pig."

185

The band came marching down the street, and they all ran along beside it. The flag was gloriously waving in front, then came the buglers blowing and the fifers tootling and the drummer rattling the drumsticks on the drum. Up the street and down the street went the band, with all the boys following it, and then it stopped in the Square by the brass cannons.

Hundreds of people were there, crowding to watch.

The cannons sat on their haunches, pointing their long barrels upward. The band kept on playing. Two men kept shouting, "Stand back! Stand back!" and other men were pouring black powder into the cannons' muzzles and pushing it down with wads of cloth on long rods.

The iron rods had two handles, and two men pushed and pulled on them, driving the black powder down the brass barrels. Then all the boys ran to pull grass and weeds along the railroad tracks. They carried them by armfuls to the cannons, and the men crowded the weeds

186

into the cannons' muzzles and drove them down with the long rods.

A bonfire was burning by the railroad tracks, and long iron rods were heating in it.

When all the weeds and grass had been packed tight against the powder in the cannons, a man took a little more powder in his hand and carefully filled the two little touchholes in the barrels. Now everybody was shouting,

"Stand back! Stand back!"

Mother took hold of Almanzo's arm and made him come away with her. He told her:

"Aw, Mother, they're only loaded with powder and weeds. I won't get hurt, Mother. I'll be careful, honest." But she made him come away from the cannons.

Two men took the long iron rods from the fire. Everybody was still, watching. Standing as far behind the cannons as they could, the two men stretched out the rods and touched their red-hot tips to the touchholes. A little flame like a candle-flame flickered up from the powder.

187

The little flames stood there burning; nobody breathed. Then—BOOM!

The cannons leaped backward, the air was full of flying grass and weeds. Almanzo ran with all the other boys to feel the warm muzzles of the cannons. Everybody was exclaiming about what a loud noise they had made.

"That's the noise that made the Redcoats run!" Mr. Paddock said to Father.

"Maybe," Father said, tugging his beard. "But it was muskets that won the Revolution. And don't forget it was axes and plows that made this country."

"That's so, come to think of it," Mr. Paddock said.

Independence Day was over. The cannons had been fired, and there was nothing more to do but hitch up the horses and drive home to do the chores.

That night when they were going to the house with the milk, Almanzo asked Father,

"Father, how was it axes and plows that made this country? Didn't we fight England for it?"

"We fought for Independence, son," Father

said. "But all the land our forefathers had was a little strip of country, here between the mountains and the ocean. All the way from here west was Indian country, and Spanish and French and English country. It was farmers that took all that country and made it America."

"How?" Almanzo asked.

"Well, son, the Spaniards were soldiers, and high-and-mighty gentlemen that only wanted gold. And the French were fur-traders, wanting to make quick money. And England was busy fighting wars. But we were farmers, son; we wanted the land. It was farmers that went over the mountains, and cleared the land, and settled it, and farmed it, and hung on to their farms.

"This country goes three thousand miles west, now. It goes 'way out beyond Kansas, and beyond the Great American Desert, over mountains bigger than these mountains, and down to the Pacific Ocean. It's the biggest country in the world, and it was farmers who took all that country and made it America, son. Don't you ever forget that."

Chapter 17

Summer-Time

THE sunshine was hotter now, and all the green things grew quickly. The corn thrust its rustling, narrow leaves waist-high; Father plowed it again, and Royal and Almanzo hoed it again. Then the corn was laid by. It had gained so much advantage against the weeds that it could hold the field with no more help.

The bushy rows of potatoes almost touched, and their white blossoms were like foam on the field. The oats rippled gray-green, and the wheat's thin heads were rough with young husks where the kernels would grow. The meadows were rosy-purple with the blossoms that the bees loved best.

Work was not so pressing now. Almanzo had time to weed the garden, and to hoe the row of potato plants he was raising from seed. He had planted a few potato seeds, just to see what they would do. And every morning he fed his pumpkin, that he was growing for the County Fair.

Father had shown him how to raise a milk-fed pumpkin. They had picked out the best vine in the field, and snipped off all the branches but one, and all the yellow pumpkin blossoms but one. Then between the root and the wee green pumpkin they carefully made a little slit on the under side of the vine. Under the slit Almanzo made a hollow in the ground and set a bowl of milk in it. Then he put a candle wick in the milk, and the end of the candle wick he put carefully into the slit.

Every day the pumpkin vine drank up the bowlful of milk, through the candle wick, and the pumpkin was growing enormously. Already it was three times as big as any other pumpkin in the field.

Almanzo had his little pig now, too. He had bought her with his half-dollar, and she was so small that he fed her, at first, with a rag dipped in milk. But soon she learned to drink. He kept her in a pen in the shade, because young pigs grow best in the shade, and he fed her all she could eat. She was growing fast, too.

So was Almanzo, but he was not growing fast enough. He drank all the milk he could hold, and at mealtimes he filled his plate so full that he could not eat it all. Father looked stern because he left food on his plate, and asked:

"What's the matter, son? Your eyes bigger than your stomach?"

Then Almanzo tried to swallow a little more. He did not tell anyone he was trying to grow up faster so he could help break the colts.

Every day Father took the two-year-olds out, one by one on a long rope, and trained them to start and to stop when he spoke. He trained them to wear bridles and harness, and not to be afraid of anything. Pretty soon he would hitch each one up with a gentle old horse, and teach it to pull a light cart behind it without being scared. But he wouldn't let Almanzo even go into the barnyard while he was training them.

Almanzo was sure he wouldn't frighten them; he wouldn't teach them to jump, or balk, or try to run away. But Father wouldn't trust a nine-year-old.

That year Beauty had the prettiest colt Almanzo had ever seen. He had a perfect white star on his forehead, and Almanzo named him Starlight. He ran in the pasture with his mother, and once when Father was in town Almanzo went into the pasture.

Beauty lifted her head and watched him coming, and the little colt ran behind her. Almanzo stopped, and stood perfectly still. After a while Starlight peeked at him, under Beauty's neck. Almanzo didn't move. Little by little the colt stretched its neck toward Almanzo, looking at him with wondering, wide eyes. Beauty nuzzled his back and switched her tail; then she took a step and bit off a clump of grass. Starlight stood trembling, looking at Almanzo. Beauty watched them both, chewing placidly. The colt made one step, then another. He was so near that Almanzo could almost have touched him, but he didn't; he didn't move. Starlight came a step nearer. Almanzo didn't even breathe. Suddenly the colt turned and ran back to its mother. Almanzo heard Eliza Jane calling:

" 'Ma-a-a-nzo!' "

She had seen him. That night she told Father. Almanzo said he hadn't done a thing, honest he hadn't, but Father said:

"Let me catch you fooling with that colt again and I'll tan your jacket. That's too good a colt to be spoiled. I won't have you teaching it tricks that I'll have to train out of it."

The summer days were long and hot now, and Mother said this was good growing weather. But Almanzo felt that everything was growing but him. Day after day went by, and nothing seemed to change. Almanzo weeded and hoed the garden, he helped mend the stone fences, he chopped wood and did the chores. In the hot afternoons when there wasn't much to do, he went swimming.

Sometimes he woke in the morning and heard rain drumming on the roof. That meant he and Father might go fishing.

He didn't dare speak to Father about fishing, because it was wrong to waste time in idleness. Even on rainy days there was plenty to do. Father might mend harness, or sharpen tools, or shave shingles. Silently Almanzo ate breakfast, knowing that Father was struggling against temptation. He was afraid Father's conscience would win.

"Well, what are you going to do today?" Mother would ask. Father might answer, slowly:

"I did lay out to cultivate the carrots and mend fence."

"You can't do that, in this rain."

"No," Father would say. After breakfast he would stand looking at the falling rain, till at last he would say:

"Well! It's too wet to work outdoors. What say we go fishing, Almanzo?"

Then Almanzo ran to get the hoe and the bait-can, and he dug worms for bait. The rain drummed on his old straw hat, it ran down his arms and back, and the mud squeezed cool between his toes. He was already sopping wet when he and Father took their rods and went down across the pasture to Trout River.

Nothing ever smelled so good as the rain on clover. Nothing ever felt so good as raindrops on Almanzo's face, and the wet grass swishing around his legs. Nothing ever sounded so pleasant as the drops pattering on the bushes along Trout River, and the rush of the water over the rocks.

They stole quietly along the bank, not making a sound, and they dropped their hooks into the pool. Father stood under a hemlock tree, and Almanzo sat under a tent of cedar boughs, and watched the raindrops dimpling the water.

Suddenly he saw a silver flash in the air. Father had hooked a trout! It slithered and gleamed through the falling rain as Father flipped it to the grassy bank. Almanzo jumped up, and remembered just in time not to shout.

Then he felt a tug at his line, the tip of his rod bent almost to the water, and he jerked it upward with all his might. A shimmering big fish came up on the end of his line! It struggled and slipped in his hands, but he got it off the hook—a beautiful speckled trout, even larger than Father's. He held it up for Father to see. Then he baited his hook and flung out his line again.

Fish always bite well when raindrops are falling on the river. Father got another one, then Almanzo got two; then Father pulled out two more, and Almanzo got another one even bigger than the first. In no time at all they had two strings of good trout. Father admired Almanzo's, and Almanzo admired Father's, and they tramped home through the clover in the rain.

They were so wet they couldn't be wetter, and their skins were glowing warm. Out in the rain, by the chopping-block at the woodpile, they cut off the heads of the fish and they scraped off the silvery scales, and they cut the fish open and stripped out their insides. The big milk-pan was full of trout, and Mother dipped them in cornmeal and fried them for dinner.

"Now this afternoon, Almanzo can help me churn," said Mother.

The cows were giving so much milk that churning must be done twice a week. Mother and the girls were tired of churning, and on rainy days Almanzo had to do it.

In the whitewashed cellar the big wooden barrel churn stood on its wooden legs, half full

of cream. Almanzo turned the handle, and the churn rocked. Inside it the cream went chug! splash, chug! splash. Almanzo had to keep rocking the churn till the chugging broke the cream into grains of butter swimming in buttermilk.

Then Almanzo drank a mug of acid-creamy buttermilk and ate cookies, while Mother skimmed out the grainy butter and washed it in the round wooden butter-bowl. She washed every bit of buttermilk out of it, then she salted it, and packed the firm golden butter in her butter-tubs.

Fishing wasn't the only summer fun. Some July evening Father would say:

"All work and no play makes Jack a dull boy. Tomorrow we'll go berrying."

Almanzo didn't say anything, but inside he was all one joyful yell.

Before dawn next day they were all riding away in the lumber-wagon, wearing their oldest clothes and taking pails and bushel baskets and a big picnic lunch. They drove far into the mountains near Lake Chateaugay, where the wild huckleberries and blueberries grew.

The woods were full of other wagons, and other families berrying. They laughed and sang, and all among the trees you could hear their talking. Every year they all met friends here, that they didn't see at any other time. But all of them were busily picking berries; they talked while they worked.

The leafy low bushes covered the ground in open spaces among the trees. Blue-black berries clustered thickly under the leaves, and there was a syrupy smell in the hot, still sunshine.

Birds had come to feast in the berry-patches; the air was aflutter with wings, and angry blue jays flew scolding at the heads of the pickers. Once two blue jays attacked Alice's sunbonnet, and Almanzo had to beat them off. And once he was picking by himself, and behind a cedar tree he met a black bear.

The bear was standing on his hind legs, stuffing berries into his mouth with both furry paws. Almanzo stood stockstill, and so did the bear. Almanzo stared, and the bear stared back at him with little, scared eyes above his motionless paws. Then the bear dropped on all fours and ran waddling away into the woods.

At noon the picnic baskets were opened by a spring, and all around in the cool shade people ate and talked. Then they drank at the spring and went back to the berry-patches.

Early in the afternoon the bushel baskets and all the pails were full, and Father drove home. They were all a little sleepy, soaked in sunshine and breathing the fruity smell of the berries.

For days Mother and the girls made jellies and jams and preserves, and for every meal there was huckleberry pie or blueberry pudding.

Then one evening at supper Father said,

"It's time Mother and I had a vacation. We're thinking of spending a week at Uncle Andrew's. Can you children take care of things and behave yourselves while we're gone?"

"I'm sure Eliza Jane and Royal can look after the place for a week," Mother said; "with Alice and Almanzo to help them."

Almanzo looked at Alice, and then they both looked at Eliza Jane. Then they all looked at Father and said:

"Yes, Father."

Chapter 18

Keeping House

UNCLE ANDREW lived ten miles away. For a week Father and Mother were getting ready to go, and all the time they were thinking of things that must be done while they were away.

Even when Mother was climbing into the buggy, she was talking.

"Be sure to gather the eggs every night," she said, "and I depend on you, Eliza Jane, to take care of the churning. Don't salt the butter too much, pack it in the small tub and be sure you cover it. Remember not to pick the beans and

203

peas I'm saving for seed. Now you all be good while we're gone —"

She was tucking her hoops down between the seat and the dashboard. Father spread the lap robe.

"—and mind, Eliza Jane. Be careful of fires; don't you leave the house while there's fire in the cookstove, and don't get to scuffling with lighted candles, whatever you do, and——"

Father tightened the reins and the horses started.

"—don't eat all the sugar!" Mother called back.

The buggy turned into the road. The horses began to trot, rapidly taking Father and Mother away. In a little while the sound of the buggy wheels ceased. Father and Mother were gone.

Nobody said anything. Even Eliza Jane looked a little scared. The house and the barns and the fields seemed very big and empty. For a whole week Father and Mother would be ten miles away.

Suddenly Almanzo threw his hat into the air and yelled. Alice hugged herself and cried:

"What'll we do first?"

They could do anything they liked. There was nobody to stop them.

"We'll do the dishes and make the beds," Eliza Jane said, bossy.

"Let's make ice-cream!" Royal shouted.

Eliza Jane loved ice-cream. She hesitated, and said, "Well——"

Almanzo ran after Royal to the ice-house. They dug a block of ice out of the sawdust and put it in a grain sack. They laid the sack on the back porch and pounded it with hatchets till the ice was crushed. Alice came out to watch them while she whipped egg-whites on a platter. She beat them with a fork, till they were too stiff to slip when she tilted the platter.

Eliza Jane measured milk and cream, and dipped up sugar from the barrel in the pantry. It was not common maple sugar, but white sugar bought from the store. Mother used it only when

205

company came. Eliza Jane dipped six cupfuls, then she smoothed the sugar that was left, and you would hardly have missed any.

She made a big milk-pail full of yellow custard. They set the pail in a tub and packed the snowy crushed ice around it, with salt, and they covered it all with a blanket. Every few minutes they took off the blanket and uncovered the pail, and stirred the freezing ice-cream.

When it was frozen, Alice brought saucers and spoons, and Almanzo brought out a cake and the butcher knife. He cut enormous pieces of cake, while Eliza Jane heaped the saucers. They could eat all the ice-cream and cake they wanted to; no one would stop them.

At noon they had eaten the whole cake, and almost all the ice-cream. Eliza Jane said it was time to get dinner, but the others didn't want any dinner. Almanzo said:

"All I want is a watermelon."

Alice jumped up. "Goody! Let's go get one!"

"Alice!" Eliza Jane cried. "You come right back here and do the breakfast dishes!"

"I will," Alice called out, "when I come back."

Alice and Almanzo went into the hot melon-field, where the melons lay round above their wilting flat leaves. Almanzo snapped his finger against the green rinds, and listened. When a melon sounded ripe, it *was* ripe, and when it sounded green, it *was* green. But when Almanzo said a melon sounded ripe, Alice thought it sounded green. There wasn't really any way to know, though Almanzo was sure he knew more about melons than any girl. So in the end they picked six of the biggest melons, and they lugged them one by one to the ice-house and put them on the damp, cold sawdust.

Then Alice went to the house to do the dishes. Almanzo said he wasn't going to do anything; maybe he'd go swimming. But as soon as Alice was out of sight, he skipped through the barns and stole into the pasture where the colts were.

The pasture was big and the sun was very hot. The air shimmered and wavered with heat, and little insects made a shrill sound. Bess and Beauty were lying down in the shade of a tree, and their little colts stood near them, waggling their small bushy tails and straddling a little on their long, gangling legs. The yearlings and the two-year-olds and the three-year-olds were grazing. All of them lifted their heads and stared at Almanzo.

He went slowly toward them, holding out his hand. There wasn't anything in his hand, but they didn't know that. He didn't mean to do anything, he only wanted to get near enough to pet them. Starlight and the other little colt ran wabbling to their mothers, and Bess and Beauty lifted up their heads and looked, then laid them down again. The big colts all pricked up their ears.

One big colt stepped toward Almanzo, then another. The six big colts were all coming. Almanzo wished he had brought carrots for them. They were so beautiful and free and big, tossing their manes and showing the whites of their eyes. The sunshine glistened on their strong, arched necks and on the muscles of their chests. Suddenly one of them said:

"Whoosh!"

One of them kicked, one of them squealed, and all at once their heads went up, their tails went up, and their hooves thundered on the ground. All their brown haunches and high black tails were turned to Almanzo. Like a thundering whirlwind those six colts went around the tree, and Almanzo heard them behind him.

He whirled around. He saw their pounding hooves and big chests coming straight at him. They were running too fast to stop. There wasn't time to get out of the way. Almanzo's eyes shut; he yelled:

"Whoa!"

The air and the ground shook. His eyes opened. He saw brown knees rising up in the air, a round belly and hind legs rushed overhead. Brown sides went by him like thunder. His hat flew off. He felt stunned. One of the three-year-olds had jumped over him. The colts were thundering down across the pasture, and Almanzo saw Royal coming.

"Leave those colts be!" Royal shouted. He

came up and said that for a cent he'd give Almanzo a licking he'd remember.

"You know better than to fool with those colts," Royal said. He took Almanzo by the ear. Almanzo trotted, but his ear was pulled all the way to the barns. He said he hadn't done anything; Royal wouldn't listen.

"Let me catch you in that pasture again and I'll whale the hide off you," Royal said. "I'll tell Father, too."

Almanzo went away, rubbing his ear. He went down to Trout River and swam in the swimming-hole till he felt better. But he thought it wasn't fair that he was the youngest in the family.

That afternoon the melons were cold, and Almanzo carried them to the grass under the balsam tree in the yard. Royal stuck the butcher knife into the dewy green rinds, and every melon was so ripe that the rinds cracked open.

Almanzo and Alice and Eliza Jane and Royal bit deep into the juicy, cold slices, and they ate till they could eat no more. Almanzo pinched the sleek black seeds, popping them at Eliza Jane until she made him quit. Then he slowly ate the last slice of melon, and he said:

"I'm going to fetch Lucy to eat up the rinds."

"You will not do any such a thing!" Eliza Jane said. "The idea! A dirty old pig in the front yard!"

"She is not, either, a dirty old pig!" said Almanzo. "Lucy's a little, young, clean pig, and pigs are the cleanest animals there are! You just ought to see the way Lucy keeps her bed clean, and turns it and airs it and makes it up every day. Horses won't do that, nor cows, nor sheep, nor anything. Pigs——"

"I guess I know that! I guess I know as much about pigs as you do!" Eliza Jane said.

"Then don't you call Lucy dirty! She's just as clean as you be!"

"Well, Mother told you to obey me," Eliza Jane answered. "And I'm not going to waste melon rinds on any pig! I'm going to make watermelon-rind preserves."

"I guess they're as much my rinds as they are

yours," Almanzo began, but Royal got up and said:

"Come along, 'Manzo. It's chore-time."

Almanzo said no more, but when the chores were done he let Lucy out of her pen. The little pig was as white as a lamb, and she liked Almanzo; her little curled tail quirked whenever she saw him. She followed him to the house, grunting happily, and she squealed for him at the door till Eliza Jane said she couldn't hear herself think.

After supper Almanzo took a plate of scraps and fed them to Lucy. He sat on the back steps and scratched her prickly back. Pigs enjoy that. In the kitchen Eliza Jane and Royal were arguing about candy. Royal wanted some, but Eliza Jane said that candy-pulls were only for winter evenings. Royal said he didn't see why candy wouldn't be just as good in the summer. Almanzo thought so, too, and he went in and sided with Royal.

Alice said she knew how to make candy. Eliza Jane wouldn't do it, but Alice mixed sugar and molasses and water, and boiled them; then she poured the candy on buttered platters and set it on the porch to cool. They rolled up their sleeves and buttered their hands, ready to pull it, and Eliza Jane buttered her hands, too.

All the time, Lucy was squealing for Almanzo. He went out to see if the candy was cool enough, and he thought his little pig should have some. The candy was cool. No one was watching, so he took a big wad of the soft, brown candy and dropped it over the edge of the porch into Lucy's wide-open mouth.

Then they all pulled candy. They pulled it into long strands, and doubled the strands, and pulled again. Every time they doubled it, they took a bite.

It was very sticky. It stuck to their teeth and their fingers and their faces, somehow it got in their hair and stuck, and when Almanzo dropped some on the floor, it stuck there. It should have become hard and brittle, but it didn't. They pulled and they pulled; still it was soft and sticky. Long past bedtime, they gave it up and went to bed.

Next morning when Almanzo started to do the chores, Lucy was standing in the yard. Her tail hung limp and her head hung down. She did not squeal when she saw him. She shook her head sadly and wrinkled her nose.

Where her white teeth should have been, there was a smooth, brown streak.

Lucy's teeth were stuck together with candy!

She could not eat, she could not drink, she could not even squeal. She could not grunt. But when she saw Almanzo coming, she ran.

Almanzo yelled for Royal. They chased Lucy all around the house, under the snowball bushes and the lilacs. They chased her all over the garden. Lucy whirled and dodged and ducked and ran like anything. All the time she didn't make a sound; she couldn't. Her mouth was full of candy.

She ran between Royal's legs and upset him. Almanzo almost grabbed her, and went sprawling on his nose. She tore through the peas, and squashed the ripe tomatoes, and uprooted the green round cabbages. Eliza Jane kept telling Royal and Almanzo to catch her. Alice ran after her.

At last they cornered her. She dashed around Alice's skirts. Almanzo fell on her and grabbed. She kicked, and tore a long hole down the front of his blouse.

Almanzo held her down. Alice held her kicking hind legs. Royal pried her mouth open and scraped out the candy. Then how Lucy

215

squealed! She squealed all the squeals that had been in her all night and all the squeals she couldn't squeal while they were chasing her, and she ran screaming to her pen.

"Almanzo James Wilder, just look at yourself!" Eliza Jane scolded. He couldn't, and he didn't want to.

Even Alice was horrified because he had wasted candy on a pig. And his blouse was ruined; it could be patched, but the patch would show.

"I don't care," Almanzo said. He was glad it was a whole week before Mother would know.

That day they made ice-cream again, and they ate the last cake. Alice said she knew how to make a pound-cake. She said she'd make one, and then she was going to go sit in the parlor.

Almanzo thought that wouldn't be any fun. But Eliza Jane said:

"You'll do no such thing, Alice. You know very well the parlor's just for company."

It was not Eliza Jane's parlor, and Mother hadn't said she couldn't sit in it. Almanzo thought that Alice could sit in the parlor if she wanted to.

That afternoon he came into the kitchen to see if the pound cake was done. Alice was taking it out of the oven. It smelled so good that he broke a little piece off the corner. Then Alice cut a slice to hide the broken place, and then they ate two more slices with the last of the ice-cream.

"I can make more ice-cream," Alice said. Eliza Jane was upstairs, and Almanzo said:

"Let's go into the parlor."

They tiptoed in, without making a sound. The light was dim because the blinds were down, but the parlor was beautiful. The wallpaper was white and gold and the carpet was of Mother's best weaving, almost too fine to step on. The center-table was marble-topped, and it held the tall parlor lamp, all white-and-gold china and pink painted roses. Beside it lay the photograph album, with covers of red velvet and mother-of-pearl.

All around the walls stood solemn horsehair chairs, and George Washington's picture looked sternly from its frame between the windows.

Alice hitched up her hoops behind, and sat on the sofa. The slippery haircloth slid her right

217

off onto the floor. She didn't dare laugh out loud, for fear Eliza Jane would hear. She sat on the sofa again, and slid off again. Then Almanzo slid off a chair.

When company came and they had to sit in the parlor, they kept themselves on the slippery chairs by pushing their toes against the floor. But now they could let go and slide. They slid off the sofa and the chairs till Alice was giggling so hard they didn't dare slide any more.

Then they looked at the shells and the coral and the little china figures on the what-not. They didn't touch anything. They looked till they heard Eliza Jane coming downstairs; then they ran tiptoe out of the parlor and shut the door without a sound. Eliza Jane didn't catch them.

It seemed that a week would last forever, but suddenly it was gone. One morning at breakfast Eliza Jane said:

"Father and Mother will be here tomorrow."

They all stopped eating. The garden had not been weeded. The peas and beans had not been picked, so the vines were ripening too soon. The henhouse had not been whitewashed.

"This house is a sight," Eliza Jane said. "And we must churn today. But what am I going to tell Mother? The sugar is all gone."

Nobody ate any more. They looked into the sugar-barrel, and they could see the bottom of it.

Only Alice tried to be cheerful.

"We must hope for the best," she said, like Mother. "There's *some* sugar left. Mother said, 'Don't eat *all* the sugar,' and we didn't. There's some around the edges."

This was only the beginning of that awful day. They all went to work as hard as they could. Royal and Almanzo hoed the garden, they whitewashed the henhouse, they cleaned the cows' stalls and swept the South-Barn Floor. The girls were sweeping and scrubbing in the house. Eliza Jane made Almanzo churn till the butter came, and her hands flew while she washed and salted it and packed it in the tub. There was only bread and butter and jam for dinner, though Almanzo was starved.

"Now, Almanzo, you polish the heater," Eliza Jane said.

He hated to polish stoves, but he hoped Eliza Jane would not tell that he had wasted candy on his pig. He went to work with the stove-blacking and the brush. Eliza Jane was hurrying and nagging.

"Be careful you don't spill the polish," she said, busily dusting.

Almanzo guessed he knew enough not to spill stove polish. But he didn't say anything.

"Use less water, Almanzo. And, mercy! rub harder than that!" He didn't say anything.

Eliza Jane went into the parlor to dust it. She called: "Almanzo, that stove done now?"

"No," said Almanzo.

"Goodness! don't dawdle so!"

Almanzo muttered, "Whose boss are you?"

Eliza Jane asked, "What's that you say?"

"Nothing," Almanzo said.

Eliza Jane came to the door. "You did so say something."

Almanzo straightened up and shouted,

"I say, *WHOSE BOSS ARE YOU?*"

Eliza Jane gasped. Then she cried out:

"You just wait, Almanzo James Wilder! You just wait till I tell Moth——"

Almanzo didn't mean to throw the blacking-brush. It flew right out of his hand. It sailed past Eliza Jane's head. Smack! it hit the parlor wall.

A great splash and smear of blacking appeared on the white-and-gold wall-paper.

Alice screamed. Almanzo turned around and ran all the way to the barn. He climbed into the haymow and crawled far back into the hay. He did not cry, but he would have cried if he hadn't been almost ten years old.

Mother would come home and find he had ruined her beautiful parlor. Father would take him into the woodshed and whip him with the blacksnake whip. He didn't want ever to come out of the haymow. He wished he could stay there forever.

After a long while Royal came into the haymow and called him. He crawled out of the hay, and he saw that Royal knew.

"Mannie, you'll get an awful whipping," Royal said. Royal was sorry, but he couldn't do anything. They both knew that Almanzo deserved whipping, and there was no way to keep Father from knowing it. So Almanzo said:

"I don't care."

He helped do the chores, and he ate supper. He wasn't hungry, but he ate to show Eliza Jane he didn't care. Then he went to bed. The parlor door was shut, but he knew how the black splotch looked on the white-and-gold wall.

Next day Father and Mother came driving into the yard. Almanzo had to go out to meet them with the others. Alice whispered to him: "Don't feel bad. Maybe they won't care." But she looked anxious, too.

Father said, cheerfully: "Well, here we are. Been getting along all right?"

"Yes, Father," Royal answered. Almanzo didn't go to help unhitch the driving-horses; he stayed in the house.

Mother hurried about, looking at everything while she untied her bonnet strings.

"I declare, Eliza Jane and Alice," she said, "you've kept the house as well as I'd have done myself."

"Mother," Alice said, in a small voice. "Mother——"

"Well, child, what is it?"

"Mother," Alice said, bravely, "you told us not to eat *all* the sugar. Mother, we—we ate almost all of it."

Mother laughed. "You've all been so good," she said, "I won't scold about the sugar."

She did not know that the black splotch was on the parlor wall. The parlor door was shut. She did not know it that day, nor all the next day. Almanzo could hardly choke down his food at mealtimes, and Mother worried. She took him into the pantry and made him swallow a big spoonful of horrible black medicine she had made of roots and herbs.

He did not want her to know about the black splotch, and yet he wished she did know. When the worst was over he could stop dreading it.

That second evening they heard a buggy driving into the yard. Mr. and Mrs. Webb were in it. Father and Mother went out to meet them and in a minute they all came into the dining-room. Almanzo heard Mother saying,

"Come right into the parlor!"

He couldn't move. He could not speak. This was worse than anything he had thought of. Mother was so proud of her beautiful parlor. She was so proud of keeping it always nice. She didn't know he had ruined it, and now she was taking company in. They would see that big black splotch on the wall.

Mother opened the parlor door and went in. Mrs. Webb went in, and Mr. Webb and Father. Almanzo saw only their backs, but he heard the window-shades going up. He saw that the parlor was full of light. It seemed to him a long time before anybody said anything.

Then Mother said:

"Take this big chair, Mr. Webb, and make yourself comfortable. Sit right here on the sofa, Mrs. Webb."

Almanzo couldn't believe his ears. Mrs. Webb said:

"You have such a beautiful parlor, I declare it's almost too fine to sit in."

Now Almanzo could see where the blacking-brush had hit the wall, and he could not believe his eyes. The wall-paper was pure white and gold. There was no black splotch.

Mother caught sight of him and said:

"Come in, Almanzo."

Almanzo went in. He sat up straight on a haircloth chair and pushed his toes against the floor to keep from sliding off. Father and Mother were telling all about the visit to Uncle Andrew's. There was no black splotch anywhere on the wall.

"Didn't you worry, leaving the children alone here and you so far away?" Mrs. Webb asked.

"No," Mother said, proudly. "I knew the children would take care of everything as well as if James and I were to home."

Almanzo minded his manners and did not say a word.

Next day, when no one was looking, he stole into the parlor. He looked carefully at the place where the black splotch had been. The wall-paper was patched. The patch had been cut out

226

carefully all around the gold scrolls, and the pattern was fitted perfectly and the edges of the patch scraped so thin that he could hardly find them.

He waited until he could speak to Eliza Jane alone, and then he asked:

"Eliza Jane, did you patch the parlor wallpaper for me?"

"Yes," she said. "I got the scraps of wallpaper that were saved in the attic, and cut out the patch and put it on with flour-paste."

Almanzo said, gruffly:

"I'm sorry I threw that brush at you. Honest, I didn't mean to, Eliza Jane."

"I guess I was aggravating," she said. "But I didn't mean to be. You're the only little brother I've got."

Almanzo had never known before how much he liked Eliza Jane.

They never, never told about the black splotch on the parlor wall, and Mother never knew.

Chapter 19

Early Harvest

NOW it was haying-time. Father brought out the scythes, and Almanzo turned the grindstone with one hand and poured a little stream of water on it with the other hand, while Father held the steel edges delicately against the whirring stone. The water kept the scythes from getting too hot, while the stone ground their edges thin and sharp.

Then Almanzo went through the woods to the little French cabins, and told French Joe and Lazy John to come to work next morning.

228

As soon as the sun dried the dew on the meadows, Father and Joe and John began cutting the hay. They walked side by side, swinging their scythes into the tall grass, and the plumed timothy fell in great swathes.

Swish! swish! swish! went the scythes, while Almanzo and Pierre and Louis followed behind them, spreading out the heavy swathes with pitchforks so that they would dry evenly in the sunshine. The stubble was soft and cool under their bare feet. Birds flew up before the mowers, now and then a rabbit jumped and bounded away. High up in the air the meadowlarks sang.

The sun grew hotter. The smell of the hay grew stronger and sweeter. Then waves of heat began to come up from the ground. Almanzo's brown arms burned browner, and sweat trickled on his forehead. The men stopped to put green leaves in the crowns of their hats, and so did the boys. For a little while the leaves were cool on top of their heads.

In the middle of the morning, Mother blew the dinner horn. Almanzo knew what that meant. He stuck his pitchfork in the ground, and went running and skipping down across the meadows to the house. Mother met him on the back porch with the milk-pail, brimming full of cold egg-nog.

The egg-nog was made of milk and cream, with plenty of eggs and sugar. Its foamy top was freckled with spices, and pieces of ice floated in it. The sides of the pail were misty with cold.

Almanzo trudged slowly toward the hayfield with the heavy pail and a dipper. He thought to himself that the pail was too full, he might spill some of the egg-nog. Mother said waste was sinful. He was sure it would be sinful to waste a drop of that egg-nog. He should do something to save it. So he set down the pail, he dipped the dipper full, and he drank. The cold egg-nog slid smoothly down his throat, and it made him cool inside.

When he reached the hayfield, everyone stopped work. They stood in the shade of an oak and pushed back their hats; and passed the dipper from hand to hand till all the egg-nog was gone. Almanzo drank his full share. The breeze seemed cool now, and Lazy John said, wiping the foam from his mustache,

"Ah! That puts heart into a man!"

Now the men whetted their scythes, making the whetstones ring gaily on the steel blades. And they went back to work with a will. Father always maintained that a man would do more work in his twelve hours, if he had a rest and all the egg-nog he could drink, morning and afternoon.

They all worked in the hayfield as long as there was light enough to see what they were doing, and the chores were done by lantern-light.

Next morning the swathes had dried, and the boys raked them into windrows, with big, light, wooden rakes that Father had made. Then Joe and John went on cutting hay, and Pierre and Louis spread the swathes behind them. But Almanzo worked on the hay-rack.

Father drove it up from the barns, and Father and Royal pitched the windrows into it, while

Almanzo trampled them down. Back and forth he ran, on the sweet-smelling hay, packing it down as fast as Father and Royal pitched it into the rack.

When the rack would hold no more he was high up in the air, on top of the load. There he lay on his stomach and kicked up his heels, while Father drove down to the Big Barn. The load of hay barely squeezed under the top of the tall doorway, and it was a long slide to the ground.

Father and Royal pitched the hay into the haymow, while Almanzo took the water-jug to the well. He pumped, then jumped and caught the gushing cold water in his hand and drank. He carried water to Father and Royal, and he filled the jug again. Then he rode back in the empty hay-rack, and trampled down another load.

Almanzo liked haying-time. From dawn till long after dark every day he was busy, always doing different things. It was like play, and morning and afternoon there was the cold egg-nog. But after three weeks of making hay, all the haymows were crammed to bursting and the meadows were bare. Then the rush of harvest-time came.

The oats were ripe, standing thick and tall and yellow. The wheat was golden, darker than the oats. The beans were ripe, and pumpkins and carrots and turnips and potatoes were ready to gather.

There was no rest and no play for anyone now. They all worked from candle-light to candle-light. Mother and the girls were making cucumber pickles, green-tomato pickles, and watermelon-rind pickles; they were drying corn and apples, and making preserves. Everything must be saved, nothing wasted of all the summer's bounty. Even the apple cores were saved for making vinegar, and a bundle of oat-straw was soaking in a tub on the back porch. Whenever Mother had one minute to spare, she braided an inch or two of oat-straw braid for making next summer's hats.

The oats were not cut with scythes, but with cradles. Cradles had blades like scythes, but they also had long wooden teeth that caught the cut stalks and held them. When they had cut enough for a bundle, Joe and John slid the stalks off in neat piles. Father and Royal and Almanzo followed behind, binding them into sheaves.

Almanzo had never bound oats before. Father showed him how to knot two handfuls of stalks into a long band, then how to gather up an armful of grain, pull the band tightly around the middle, twist its ends together, and tuck them in tightly.

In a little while he could bind a sheaf pretty well, but not very fast. Father and Royal could bind oats as fast as the reapers cut them.

Just before sunset the reapers stopped reaping, and they all began shocking the sheaves. All the cut oats must be shocked before dark, because they would spoil if they lay on the ground in the dew overnight.

Almanzo could shock oats as well as anybody. He stood ten sheaves up on their stem ends, close together with all the heads of grain upward. Then he set two more sheaves on top and spread out their stems to make a roof over the ten sheaves. The shocks looked like little Indian wigwams, dotted all over the field of pale stubble.

The wheat-field was waiting; there was no time to lose. As soon as all the oats were in the shock, everyone hurried to cut and bind and shock the wheat. It was harder to handle because it was heavier than the oats, but Almanzo manfully did his best. Then there was the field of oats and Canada peas. The pea vines were tangled all through the oats, so they could not

be shocked. Almanzo raked them into long windrows.

Already it was high time to pull the navy beans. Alice had to help with them. Father hauled the bean-stakes to the field and set them up, driving them into the ground with a maul. Then Father and Royal hauled the shocked grain to the barns, while Almanzo and Alice pulled the beans.

First they laid rocks all around the bean-stakes, to keep the beans off the ground. Then they pulled up the beans. With both hands they pulled till their hands could hold no more. They carried the beans to the stakes and laid the roots against them, spreading the long vines out on the rocks.

Layer after layer of beans they piled around each stake. The roots were bigger than the vines, so the pile grew higher and higher in the middle. The tangled vines, full of rattling bean-pods, hung down all around.

When the roots were piled to the tops of the stakes, Almanzo and Alice laid vines over the

236

top, making a little roof to shed rain. Then that bean-stake was done, and they began another one.

The stakes were as tall as Almanzo, and the vines stood out around them like Alice's hoop-skirts.

One day when Almanzo and Alice came to dinner, the butter-buyer was there. He came every year from New York City. He wore fine city clothes, with a gold watch and chain, and he drove a good team. Everybody liked the butter-buyer, and dinner-time was exciting when he was there. He brought all the news of politics and fashions and prices in New York City.

After dinner Almanzo went back to work, but Alice stayed to watch Mother sell the butter.

The butter-buyer went down cellar, where the butter-tubs stood covered with clean white cloths. Mother took off the cloths, and the butter-buyer pushed his long steel butter-tester down through the butter, to the bottom of the tub.

The butter-tester was hollow, with a slit in

one side. When he pulled it out, there in the slit was the long sample of butter.

Mother did not do any bargaining at all. She said, proudly:

"My butter speaks for itself."

Not one sample from all her tubs had a streak in it. From top to bottom of every tub, Mother's butter was all the same golden, firm, sweet butter.

Almanzo saw the butter-buyer drive away, and Alice came skipping to the beanfield, swinging her sunbonnet by its strings. She called out:

"Guess what he did!"

"What?" Almanzo asked.

"He said Mother's butter is the best butter he ever saw anywhere! And he paid her—Guess what he paid her! Fifty—cents—a—pound!"

Almanzo was amazed. He had never heard of such a price for butter.

"She had five hundred pounds!" Alice said. "That's two hundred and fifty dollars! He paid her all that money, and she's hitching up right now, to take it to the bank."

238

In a little while Mother drove away, in her second-best bonnet and her black bombazine. She was going to town in the afternoon, on a week-day in harvest-time. She had never done such a thing before. But Father was busy in the fields, and she would not keep all that money in the house overnight.

Almanzo was proud. His Mother was probably the best butter-maker in the whole of New York State. People in New York City would eat it, and say to one another how good it was, and wonder who made it.

Chapter 20

Late Harvest

NOW the harvest moon shone round and yellow over the fields at night, and there was a frosty chill in the air. All the corn was cut and stood in tall shocks. The moon cast their black shadows on the ground where the pumpkins lay naked above their withered leaves.

Almanzo's milk-fed pumpkin was enormous. He cut it carefully from the vine, but he could not lift it; he could not even roll it over. Father lifted it into the wagon and carefully hauled it

240

to the barn and laid it on some hay to wait till County Fair time.

All the other pumpkins Almanzo rolled into piles, and Father hauled them to the barns. The best ones were put in the cellar to make pumpkin pies, and the rest were piled on the South-Barn Floor. Every night Almanzo cut up some of them with a hatchet, and fed them to the cows and calves and oxen.

The apples were ripe. Almanzo and Royal and Father set ladders against the trees, and climbed into the leafy tops. They picked every perfect apple carefully, and laid it in a basket. Father drove the wagonful of baskets slowly to the house, and Almanzo helped carry the baskets down cellar and lay the apples carefully in the apple-bins. They didn't bruise one apple, for a bruised apple will rot, and one rotten apple will spoil a whole bin.

The cellar began to have its winter smell of apples and preserves. Mother's milk-pans had been moved upstairs to the pantry, till spring came again.

After the perfect apples had all been picked, Almanzo and Royal could shake the trees. That was fun. They shook the trees with all their might, and the apples came rattling down like hail. They picked them up and threw them into the wagon; they were only cider-apples. Almanzo took a bite out of one whenever he wanted to.

Now it was time to gather the garden-stuff. Father hauled the apples away to the cider-mill, but Almanzo had to stay at home, pulling beets and turnips and parsnips and carrying them down cellar. He pulled the onions and Alice braided their dry tops in long braids. The round onions hung thick on both sides of the braids, and Mother hung them in the attic. Almanzo pulled the pepper-plants, while Alice threaded her darning-needle and strung the red peppers like beads on a string. They were hung up beside the onions.

Father came back that night with two big hogsheads of cider. He rolled them down cellar. There was plenty of cider to last till next apple-harvest.

Next morning a cold wind was blowing, and storm clouds were rolling up against a gray sky. Father looked worried. The carrots and potatoes must be dug, quickly.

Almanzo put on his socks and moccasins, his cap and coat and mittens, and Alice put on her hood and shawl. She was going to help.

Father hitched Bess and Beauty to the plow, and turned a furrow away from each side of the long rows of carrots. That left the carrots standing in a thin ridge of earth, so they were easy to pull. Almanzo and Alice pulled them as fast as they could, and Royal cut off the feathery tops and threw the carrots in the wagon. Father hauled them to the house and shoveled them down a chute into the carrot-bins in the cellar.

The little red seeds that Almanzo and Alice planted had grown into two hundred bushels of carrots. Mother could cook all she wanted, and the horses and cows could eat raw carrots all winter.

Lazy John came to help with the potato-digging. Father and John dug the potatoes with hoes, while Alice and Almanzo picked them up, put them in baskets, and emptied the baskets into a wagon. Royal left an empty wagon in the field while he hauled the full one to the house and shoveled the potatoes through the cellar window into the potato bins. Almanzo and Alice hurried to fill the empty wagon while he was gone.

They hardly stopped at noon to eat. They worked at night until it was too dark to see. If they didn't get the potatoes into the cellar before the ground froze, all the year's work in the potato-field would be lost. Father would have to buy potatoes.

"I never saw such weather for the time of year," Father said.

Early in the morning, before the sun rose, they were hard at work again. The sun did not rise at all. Thick gray clouds hung low overhead. The ground was cold and the potatoes were cold, and a sharp, cold wind blew gritty dust into Almanzo's eyes. He and Alice were sleepy. They tried to hurry, but their fingers were so cold that they fumbled and dropped potatoes. Alice said:

"My nose is so cold. We have ear-muffs. Why can't we have nose-muffs?"

Almanzo told Father that they were cold, and Father told him:

"Get a hustle on, son. Exercise'll keep you warm."

They tried, but they were too cold to hustle very fast. The next time Father came digging near them, he said:

"Make a bonfire of the dry potato-tops, Almanzo. That will warm you."

So Alice and Almanzo gathered an enormous pile of potato-tops. Father gave Almanzo a match, and he lighted the bonfire. The little flame grabbed a dry leaf, then it ran eagerly up a stem, and it crackled and spread and rushed roaring into the air. It seemed to make the whole field warmer.

For a long time they all worked busily. Whenever Almanzo was too cold, he ran and piled more potato tops on the fire. Alice held out her grubby hands to warm them, and the fire shone on her face like sunshine.

"I'm hungry," Almanzo said.

"So be I," said Alice. "It must be almost dinner-time."

Almanzo couldn't tell by the shadows, because there was no sunshine. They worked and they worked, and still they did not hear the dinner horn. Almanzo was all hollow inside. He said to Alice:

"Before we get to the end of this row, we'll hear it." But they didn't. Almanzo decided something must have happened to the horn. He said to Father:

"I guess it's dinner-time."

John laughed at him, and Father said:

"It's hardly the middle of the morning, son."

Almanzo went on picking up potatoes. Then Father called, "Put a potato in the ashes, Almanzo. That'll take the edge off your appetite."

Almanzo put two big potatoes in the hot ashes, one for him and one for Alice. He piled hot ashes over them, and he piled more potato tops on the fire. He knew he should go back to work, but he stood in the pleasant heat, waiting for the potatoes to bake. He did not feel comfortable in his mind, but he felt warm outside, and he said to himself:

"I have to stay here to roast the potatoes."

He felt bad because he was letting Alice work all alone, but he thought:

"I'm busy roasting a potato for her."

Suddenly he heard a soft, hissing puff, and something hit his face. It stuck on his face, scalding hot. He yelled and yelled. The pain was terrible and he could not see.

He heard shouts, and running. Big hands snatched his hands from his face, and Father's hands tipped back his head. Lazy John was talking French and Alice was crying, "Oh, Father! Oh, Father!"

"Open your eyes, son," Father said.

Almanzo tried, but he could get only one open. Father's thumb pushed up the other eyelid, and it hurt. Father said:

"It's all right. The eye's not hurt."

247

One of the roasting potatoes had exploded, and the scalding-hot inside of it had hit Almanzo. But the eyelid had closed in time. Only the eyelid and his cheek were burned.

Father tied his handkerchief over the eye, and he and Lazy John went back to work.

Almanzo hadn't known that anything could hurt like that burn. But he told Alice that it didn't hurt—much. He took a stick and dug the other potato out of the ashes.

"I guess it's your potato," he snuffled. He was not crying; only tears kept running out of his eyes and down inside his nose.

"No, it's yours," Alice said. "It was my potato that exploded."

"How do you know which it was?" Almanzo asked.

"This one's yours because you're hurt, and I'm not hungry, anyway not very hungry," said Alice.

"You're as hungry as I be!" Almanzo said. He could not bear to be selfish any more. "You eat half," he told Alice, "and I'll eat half."

248

The potato was burned black outside, but inside it was white and mealy and a most delicious baked-potato smell steamed out of it. They let it cool a little, and then they gnawed the inside out of the black crust, and it was the best potato they had ever eaten. They felt better and went back to work.

Almanzo's face was blistered and his eye was swelled shut. But Mother put a poultice on it at noon, and another at night, and next day it did not hurt so much.

Just after dark on the third day, he and Alice followed the last load of potatoes to the house.

The weather was growing colder every minute. Father shoveled the potatoes into the cellar by lantern-light, while Royal and Almanzo did all the chores.

They had barely saved the potatoes. That very night the ground froze.

"A miss is as good as a mile," Mother said, but Father shook his head.

"Too close to suit me," he said. "Next thing will be snow. We'll have to hustle to get the beans and the corn under cover."

He put the hay-rack on the wagon, and Royal and Almanzo helped him haul the beans. They pulled up the bean-stakes and laid them in the wagon, beans and all. They worked carefully, for a jar would shake the beans out of the dry pods and waste them.

When they had piled all the beans on the South-Barn Floor, they hauled in the shocks of corn. The crops had been so good that even Father's great barn-roofs would not shelter all the harvest. Several loads of corn-shocks had to be put in the barnyard, and Father made a fence around them to keep them safe from the young cattle.

All the harvest was in, now. Cellar and attic and the barns were stuffed to bursting. Plenty of food, and plenty of feed for all the stock, was stored away for the winter.

Everyone could stop working for a while, and have a good time at the County Fair.

Chapter 21

County Fair

EARLY in the frosty morning they all set out for the Fair. All of them were dressed up in their Sunday clothes except Mother. She wore her second-best and took an apron, for she was going to help with the church dinner.

Under the back buggy-seat was the box of jellies and pickles and preserves that Eliza Jane and Alice had made to show at the Fair. Alice was taking her woolwork embroidery, too. But Almanzo's milk-fed pumpkin had gone the day before.

It was too big to go in the buggy. Almanzo had polished it carefully, Father had lifted it into the wagon and rolled it onto a soft pile of hay, and they had taken it to the Fair Grounds and given it to Mr. Paddock. Mr. Paddock was in charge of such things.

This morning the roads were lively with people driving to the Fair, and in Malone the crowds were thicker than they had been on Independence Day. All around the Fair Grounds were acres of wagons and buggies, and people were clustered like flies. Flags were flying and the band was playing.

Mother and Royal and the girls got out of the buggy at the Fair Grounds, but Almanzo rode on with Father to the church sheds, and helped unhitch the horses. The sheds were full, and all along the sidewalks streams of people in their best clothes were walking to the Fair, while buggies dashed up and down the streets in clouds of dust.

"Well, son," Father asked him, "what shall we do first?"

"I want to see the horses," Almanzo said. So

Father said they would look at the horses first.

The sun was high now, and the day was clear and pleasantly warm. Streams of people were pouring into the Fair Grounds, with a great noise of talking and walking, and the band was playing gaily. Buggies were coming and going; men stopped to speak to Father, and boys were everywhere. Frank went by with some of the town boys, and Almanzo saw Miles Lewis and Aaron Webb. But he stayed with Father.

They went slowly past the tall back of the grand-stand, and past the low, long church building. This was not the church, but a church kitchen and dining-room at the Fair Grounds. A noise of dishes and rattling pans and a chatter of women's voices came out of it. Mother and the girls were inside it somewhere.

Beyond it was a row of stands, and booths, and tents, all gay with flags and colored pictures, and men shouting:

"Step this way, step this way, only ten cents, one dime, the tenth part of a dollar!" "Oranges,

oranges, sweet Florida oranges!" "Cures all ills of man and beast!" "Prizes for all! Prizes for all!" "Last call, boys, put down your money! Step back, don't crowd!"

One stand was a forest of striped black-and-white canes. If you could throw a ring over a cane, the man would give it to you. There were piles of oranges, and trays of gingerbread, and tubs of pink lemonade. There was a man in a tail coat and a tall shining hat, who put a pea under a shell and then paid money to any man who would tell him where the pea was.

"I know where it is, Father!" Almanzo said.

"Be you sure?" Father asked.

"Yes," said Almanzo, pointing. "Under that one."

"Well, son, we'll wait and see," Father said.

Just then a man pushed through the crowd and laid down a five-dollar bill beside the shells. There were three shells. The man pointed to the same shell that Almanzo had pointed at.

The man in the tall hat picked up the shell. There was no pea under it. The next instant

255

the five-dollar bill was in his tail-coat pocket, and he was showing the pea again and putting it under another shell.

Almanzo couldn't understand it. He had seen the pea under that shell, and then it wasn't there. He asked Father how the man had done it.

"I don't know, Almanzo," Father said. "But he knows. It's his game. Never bet your money on another man's game."

They went on to the stock-sheds. The ground there was trodden into deep dust by the crowd of men and boys. It was quiet there.

Almanzo and Father looked for a long time at the beautiful bay and brown and chestnut Morgan horses, with their flat, slender legs and small, neat feet. The Morgans tossed their small heads and their eyes were soft and bright. Almanzo looked at them all carefully, and not one was a better horse than the colts Father had sold last fall.

Then he and Father looked at the thorough-breds, with their longer bodies and thinner necks and slim haunches. The thoroughbreds were nervous; their ears quivered and their eyes showed the whites. They looked faster than the Morgans, but not so steady.

Beyond them were three large, speckled gray horses. Their haunches were round and hard, their necks were thick and their legs were heavy. Long, bushy hair hid their big feet. Their heads were massive, their eyes quiet and kind. Almanzo had never seen anything like them.

Father said they were Belgians. They came from a country called Belgium, in Europe. Belgium was next to France, and the French had brought such horses in ships to Canada. Now Belgian horses were coming from Canada into the United States. Father admired them very much. He said,

"Look at that muscle! They'd pull a barn, if hitched to it."

Almanzo asked him:

"What's the good of a horse than can pull a barn? We don't want to pull a barn. A Morgan has muscle enough to pull a wagon, and he's fast enough to pull a buggy, too."

257

"You're right, son!" Father said. He looked regretfully at the big horses, and shook his head. "It would be a waste to feed all that muscle, and we've got no use for it. You're right."

Almanzo felt important and grown-up, talking horses with Father.

Beyond the Belgians, a crowd of men and boys was so thick around a stall that not even Father could see what was in it. Almanzo left Father, and wriggled and squeezed between the legs until he came to the bars of the stall.

Inside it were two black creatures. He had never seen anything like them. They looked something like horses, but they were not horses. Their tails were bare, with only a bunch of hair at the tip. Their short, bristly manes stood up straight and stiff. Their ears were like rabbits' ears. Those long ears stood up above their long, gaunt faces, and while Almanzo stared, one of those creatures pointed its ears at him and stretched out its neck.

Close to Almanzo's bulging eyes, its nose wrinkled and its lips curled back from long, yellow teeth. Almanzo couldn't move. Slowly

258

the creature opened its long, fanged mouth, and out of its throat came a squawking roar.

"Eeeeeeeee, aw! Heeeeeee, Haw!"

Almanzo yelled, and he turned and butted and clawed and fought through the crowd toward Father. The next thing he knew, he reached Father, and everybody was laughing at him. Only Father did not laugh.

"It's only a half-breed horse, son," Father said. "The first mule you ever saw. You're not the only one that was scared, either," said Father, looking around at the crowd.

Almanzo felt better when he saw the colts. There were two-year-olds, and yearlings, and some little colts with their mothers. Almanzo looked at them carefully, and finally he said:

"Father, I wish——"

"What, son?" Father asked.

"Father, there's not a colt here that can hold a candle to Starlight. Couldn't you bring Starlight to the Fair next year?"

"Well, well," Father said. "We'll see about that when next year comes."

Then they looked at the cattle. There were

259

fawn-colored Guernseys and Jerseys, that come from islands named Guernsey and Jersey, near the coast of France. They looked at the bright-red Devons and the gray Durhams that come from England. They looked at young steers and yearlings, and some were finer than Star and Bright. They looked at the sturdy, powerful yoke-oxen.

All the time Almanzo was thinking that if only Father would bring Starlight to the Fair, Starlight would be sure to take a prize.

Then they looked at the big Chester White hogs, and the smoother, smaller, black Berkshire hogs. Almanzo's pig Lucy was a Chester White. But he decided that some day he would have a Berkshire, too.

They looked at Merino sheep, like Father's, with their wrinkled skins and short, fine wool, and they looked at the larger Cotswold sheep, whose wool is longer, but coarse. Father was satisfied with his Merinos; he would rather raise less wool, of finer quality, for Mother to weave.

By this time it was noon, and Almanzo had

not seen his pumpkin yet. But he was hungry, so they went to dinner.

The church dining-room was already crowded. Every place at the long table was taken, and Eliza Jane and Alice were hurrying with the other girls who were bringing loaded plates from the kitchen. All the delicious smells made Almanzo's mouth water.

Father went into the kitchen, and so did Almanzo. It was full of women, hurriedly slicing boiled hams and roasts of beef, and carving roast chickens and dishing up vegetables. Mother opened the oven of the huge cookstove and took out roasted turkeys and ducks.

Three barrels stood by the wall, and long iron pipes went into them from a caldron of water boiling on the stove. Steam puffed from every crevice of the barrels. Father pried off the cover of one barrel, and clouds of steam came out. Almanzo looked into the barrel, and it was full of steaming potatoes, in their clean brown skins. The skins broke when the air struck them, and curled back from the mealy insides.

All around Almanzo were cakes and pies of every kind, and he was so hungry he could have eaten them all. But he dared not touch even a crumb.

At last he and Father got places at the long table in the dining-room. Everyone was merry, talking and laughing, but Almanzo simply ate. He ate ham and chicken and turkey, and dressing and cranberry jelly; he ate potatoes and gravy, succotash, baked beans and boiled beans and onions, and white bread and rye'n'injun bread, and sweet pickles and jam and preserves. Then he drew a long breath, and he ate pie.

When he began to eat pie, he wished he had eaten nothing else. He ate a piece of pumpkin pie and a piece of custard pie, and he ate almost a piece of vinegar pie. He tried a piece of mince pie, but could not finish it. He just couldn't do it. There were berry pies and cream pies and vinegar pies and raisin pies, but he could not eat any more.

He was glad to sit down with Father in the grand-stand. They watched the trotting-horses flashing by, warming up for the races. Little puffs of dust rose in the sunshine behind the fast sulkies. Royal was with the big boys, down at the edge of the track, with the men who were betting on the races.

Father said it was all right to bet on races, if you wanted to.

"You get a run for your money," he said. "But I would rather get something more substantial for mine."

The grand-stand filled up till people were packed in all the tiers of seats. The light sulkies were lined up in a row, and the horses tossed their heads and pawed the ground, eager to start. Almanzo was so excited he could hardly sit still. He picked the horse he thought would win, a slim, bright chestnut thoroughbred.

Somebody shouted. All at once the horses were flying down the track, the crowd was one roaring yell. Then suddenly everyone was still, in astonishment.

An Indian was running down the track behind the sulkies. He was running as fast as the horses.

Everybody began to shout. "He can't do it!"
"Two dollars he'll keep up!" "The bay! The
bay! Come on, come on!" "Three dollars on
the Indian!" "Watch that chestnut!" "Look
at the Indian!"

The dust was blowing on the other side of

264

the track. The horses were flying, stretched out above the ground. All the crowd was up on the benches, yelling. Almanzo yelled and yelled. Down the track the horses came pounding. "Come on! Come on! The bay! The bay!"

They flashed past too quickly to be seen. Behind came the Indian, running easily. In front

265

of the grand-stand he leaped high in the air, turned a handspring, and stood, saluting all the people with his right arm.

The grand-stand shook with the noise of shouting and stamping. Even Father was shouting, "Hurrah! Hurrah!"

The Indian had run that mile in two minutes and forty seconds, as fast as the winning horse. He was not even panting. He saluted all the cheering people again, and walked off the track.

The bay horse had won.

There were more races, but soon it was three o'clock, time to go home. Driving home was exciting that day, because there was so much to talk about. Royal had thrown a ring over one of the black-and-white-striped canes, and he had it. Alice had spent a nickel for peppermint candy. She broke the striped stick in two, and each had a piece to suck slowly.

It seemed strange to be at home only long enough to do the chores and sleep. Early next morning they were driving away again. There were two more days of the Fair.

This morning Almanzo and Father went quickly past the stocksheds to the display of vegetables and grains. Almanzo caught sight of the pumpkins at once. They shone out brightly, golden among all the duller things. And there was Almanzo's pumpkin, the largest of them all.

"Don't be too sure of getting the prize, son," Father said. "It isn't size that counts as much as quality."

Almanzo tried not to care too much about the prize. He went away from the pumpkins with Father, though he couldn't help looking back at his pumpkin now and then. He saw the fine potatoes, the beets, turnips, rutabagas, and onions. He fingered the brown, plump kernels of wheat, and the grooved, pale oats, the Canada peas and navy beans and speckled beans. He looked at ears of white corn and yellow corn, and red-white-and-blue corn. Father pointed out how closely the kernels grew on the best ears, how they covered even the tip of the cob.

People walked slowly up and down, looking. There were always some people looking at the

267

pumpkins, and Almanzo wished they knew that the biggest pumpkin was his.

After dinner he hurried back to watch the judging. The crowds were larger now, and sometimes he had to leave Father and squirm between people to see what the judges were doing. The three judges wore badges on their coats; they were solemn, and talked together in low voices so that no one heard what they said.

They weighed the grains in their hands, and looked at them closely. They chewed a few grains of wheat and of oats, to see how they tasted. They split open peas and beans, and they shelled a few kernels off each ear of corn to make sure how long the kernels were. With their jack-knives they cut the onions in two, and the potatoes. They cut very thin slices of the potatoes and held them up to the light. The best part of a potato is next to the skin, and you can see how thick the best part is, if you hold a very thin slice to the light and look through it.

The thickest crowd pressed around the table where the judges were, and watched without

268

saying anything. There wasn't a sound, when at last the tall, thin judge with the chin whiskers took a snip of red ribbon and a snip of blue ribbon out of his pocket. The red ribbon was second prize, the blue one was first prize. The judge put them on the vegetables that had won them, and the crowd breathed a long breath.

Then all at once everybody talked. Almanzo saw that people who didn't get any prize, and the person who got second prize, all congratulated the winner. If his pumpkin didn't get a prize, he would have to do that. He didn't want to, but he guessed he must.

At last the judges came to the pumpkins. Almanzo tried to look as if he didn't care much, but he felt hot all over.

The judges had to wait till Mr. Paddock brought them a big, sharp butcher knife. The biggest judge took it, and thrust it with all his might into a pumpkin. He bore down hard on the handle, and cut a thick slice out. He held it up, and all the judges looked at the thick, yellow flesh of the pumpkin. They looked at the

269

thickness of the hard rind, and at the little hollow where the seeds were. They cut tiny slices, and tasted them.

Then the big judge cut open another pumpkin. He had begun with the smallest. The crowd pressed tight against Almanzo. He had to open his mouth to get his breath.

At last the judge cut open Almanzo's big pumpkin. Almanzo felt dizzy. The inside of his pumpkin had a big hollow for seeds, but it was a big pumpkin; it had lots of seeds. Its flesh was a little paler than the other pumpkins. Almanzo didn't know whether that made any difference or not. The judges tasted it; he could not tell from their faces how it tasted.

Then they talked together for a long time. He could not hear what they said. The tall, thin judge shook his head and tugged his chin whiskers. He cut a thin slice from the yellowest pumpkin and a thin slice from Almanzo's pumpkin, and tasted them. He gave them to the big judge, and he tasted them. The fat judge said something, and they all smiled.

Mr. Paddock leaned over the table and said:

"Good afternoon, Wilder. You and the boy are taking in the sight, I see. Having a good time, Almanzo?"

Almanzo could hardly speak. He managed to say: "Yes, sir."

The tall judge had taken the red ribbon and the blue ribbon out of his pocket. The fat judge took hold of his sleeve, and all the judges put their heads together again.

The tall judge turned around slowly. Slowly he took a pin from his lapel and stuck it through the blue ribbon. He was not very near Almanzo's big pumpkin. He was not near enough to reach it. He held out the blue ribbon, above another pumpkin. He leaned, and stretched out his arm slowly, and he thrust the pin into Almanzo's pumpkin.

Father's hand clapped on Almanzo's shoulder. All at once Almanzo could breathe, and he was tingling all over. Mr. Paddock was shaking his hand. All the judges were smiling. Ever so many people said, "Well, well, Mr. Wilder, so your boy's got first prize!"

Mr. Webb said, "That's a fine pumpkin, Almanzo. Don't know as I ever saw a finer."

Mr. Paddock said:

"I never saw a pumpkin that beat it for size. How'd you raise such a big pumpkin, Almanzo?"

Suddenly everything seemed big and very still. Almanzo felt cold and small and scared. He hadn't thought, before, that maybe it wasn't fair to get a prize for a milk-fed pumpkin. Maybe the prize was for raising pumpkins in the ordinary way. Maybe, if he told, they'd take the prize away from him. They might think he had tried to cheat.

He looked at Father, but Father's face didn't tell him what to do.

"I—I just—I kept hoeing it, and—" he said. Then he knew he was telling a lie. Father was hearing him tell a lie. He looked up at Mr. Paddock and said: "I raised it on milk. It's a milk-fed pumpkin. Is—is that all right?"

"Yes, that's all right," Mr. Paddock answered.

Father laughed, "There's tricks in all trades but ours, Paddock. And maybe a few tricks in farming and wagon-making, too, eh?"

Then Almanzo knew how foolish he had been. Father knew all about the pumpkin, and Father wouldn't cheat.

Afterward he went walking with Father

among the crowds. They saw the horses again, and the colt that won the prize was not so good as Starlight. Almanzo did hope that Father would bring Starlight to the Fair next year. Then they watched the foot-races, and the jumping contests, and the throwing contests. Malone boys were in them, but the farmer boys won, almost every time. Almanzo kept remembering his prize pumpkin and feeling good.

Driving home that night, they all felt good. Alice's woolwork had won first prize, and Eliza Jane had a red ribbon and Alice had a blue ribbon for jellies. Father said the Wilder family had done itself proud, that day.

There was another day of the Fair, but it wasn't so much fun. Almanzo was tired of having a good time. Three days of it were too much. It didn't seem right to be dressed up again and leaving the farm. He felt unsettled, as he did at house-cleaning time. He was glad when the Fair was over and everything could go on as usual.

Chapter 22

Fall of the Year

"WIND'S in the north," Father said at breakfast. "And clouds coming up. We better get
the beechnuts in before it snows."

The beech trees grew in the timber lot, two
miles away by the road, but only half a mile
across the fields. Mr. Webb was a good neigh-
bor, and let Father drive across his land.

Almanzo and Royal put on their caps and
warm coats, Alice put on her cloak and hood,
and they rode away with Father in the wagon,
to gather the beechnuts.

When they came to a stone fence Almanzo helped to take it down and let the wagon through. The pastures were empty now; all the stock was in the warm barns, so they could leave the fences down until the last trip home.

In the beech grove all the yellow leaves had fallen. They lay thick on the ground beneath the slim trunks and delicate bare limbs of the beeches. The beechnuts had fallen after the leaves and lay on top of them. Father and Royal lifted the matted leaves carefully on their pitchforks and put them, nuts and all, into the wagon. And Alice and Almanzo ran up and down in the wagon, trampling down the rustling leaves to make room for more.

When the wagon was full, Royal drove away with Father to the barns, but Almanzo and Alice stayed to play till the wagon came back.

A chill wind was blowing and the sunlight was hazy. Squirrels frisked about, storing away nuts for the winter. High in the sky the wild ducks were honking, hurrying south. It was a wonderful day for playing wild Indian, all among the trees.

When Almanzo was tired of playing Indian, he and Alice sat on a log and cracked beech-nuts in their teeth. Beechnuts are three-cornered and shiny-brown and small, but every shell is solidly full of nut. They are so good that nobody could ever eat enough of them. At least, Almanzo never got tired of eating them before the wagon came back.

Then he and Alice trampled down leaves again, while the busy pitchforks made the patch of bare ground larger and larger.

It took almost all day to gather all the beech-nuts. In the cold twilight Almanzo helped to lay up the stone fences behind the last load. All the beechnuts in their leaves made a big pile on the South-Barn Floor, beside the fanning-mill.

That night Father said they'd seen the last of Indian summer.

"It will snow tonight," he said. Sure enough, when Almanzo woke next morning the light had a snowy look, and from the window he saw the ground and the barn roofs white with snow.

Father was pleased. The soft snow was six inches deep, but the ground was not yet frozen.

"Poor man's fertilizer," Father called such a snow, and he set Royal to plowing it into all the fields. It carried something from the air into the ground, that would make the crops grow.

Meanwhile Almanzo helped Father. They tightened the barn's wooden windows, and nailed down every board that had loosened in the summer's sun and rain. They banked the walls of the barn with straw from the stalls, and they banked the walls of the house with clean, bright straw. They laid stones on the straw to hold it snug against winds. They fitted storm doors and storm windows on the house, just in time. That week ended with the first hard freeze.

Bitter cold weather had come to stay, and now it was butchering-time.

In the cold dawn, before breakfast, Almanzo helped Royal set up the big iron caldron near the barn. They set it on stones, and filled it

278

with water, and lighted a bonfire under it. It held three barrels of water.

Before they had finished, Lazy John and French Joe had come, and there was time to snatch only a bite of breakfast. Five hogs and a yearling beef were to be killed that day.

As soon as one was killed, Father and Joe and John dipped the carcass into the boiling caldron, and heaved it out and laid it on boards. With butcher knives they scraped all the hair off it. Then they hung it up by the hind feet in a tree, and cut it open and took all the insides out into a tub.

Almanzo and Royal carried the tub to the kitchen, and Mother and the girls washed the heart and liver, and snipped off all the bits of fat from the hog's insides, to make lard.

Father and Joe skinned the beef carefully. The hide came off in one big piece. Every year Father killed a beef and saved the hide to make shoes.

All that afternoon the men were cutting up the meat, and Almanzo and Royal were hurrying to put it away. All the pieces of fat pork they packed in salt, in barrels down cellar. The hams and shoulders they slid carefully into barrels of brown pork-pickle, which Mother had made of salt, maple sugar, saltpeter, and water, boiled together. Pork-pickle had a stinging smell that felt like a sneeze.

Spareribs, backbones, hearts, livers, tongues, and all the sausagemeat had to go into the woodshed attic. Father and Joe hung the quarters of beef there, too. The meat would freeze in the attic, and stay frozen all winter.

Butchering was finished that night. French Joe and Lazy John went whistling home, with fresh meat to pay for their work, and Mother baked spareribs for supper. Almanzo loved to gnaw the meat from the long, curved, flat bones. He liked the brown pork-gravy, too, on the creamy mashed potatoes.

All the next week Mother and the girls were hard at work, and Mother kept Almanzo in the kitchen to help. They cut up the pork fat and boiled it in big kettles on the stove. When it was done, Mother strained the clear hot lard through white cloths into big stone jars.

Crumbling brown cracklings were left inside the cloth after Mother squeezed it, and Almanzo sneaked a few and ate them whenever he could. Mother said they were too rich for him. She put them away to be used for seasoning cornbread.

Then she made the headcheese. She boiled the six heads till the meat came off the bones; she chopped it and seasoned it and mixed it with liquor from the boiling, and poured it into six-quart pans. When it was cold it was like jelly, for a gelatine had come out of the bones.

Next Mother made mincemeat. She boiled the best bits of beef and pork and chopped them fine. She mixed in raisins and spices, sugar and vinegar, chopped apples and brandy, and she packed two big jars full of mincemeat. It smelled delicious, and she let Almanzo eat the scraps left in the mixing-bowl.

All this time he was grinding sausagemeat. He poked thousands of pieces of meat into the

grinder and turned the handle round and round, for hours and hours. He was glad when that was finished. Mother seasoned the meat and molded it into big balls, and Almanzo had to carry all those balls into the woodshed attic and pile them up on clean cloths. They would be there, frozen, all winter, and every morning Mother would mold one ball into little cakes and fry them for breakfast.

282

The end of butchering-time was candle-making.

Mother scrubbed the big lard-kettles and filled them with bits of beef fat. Beef fat doesn't make lard; it melts into tallow. While it was melting, Almanzo helped string the candle-molds.

A candle-mold was two rows of tin tubes, fastened together and standing straight up on six feet. There were twelve tubes in a mold. They were open at the top, but tapered to a point at the bottom, and in each point there was a tiny hole.

Mother cut a length of candle-wicking for each tube. She doubled the wicking across a small stick, and twisted it into a cord. She licked her thumb and finger, and rolled the end of the cord into a sharp point. When she had six cords on the stick, she dropped them into six tubes, and the stick lay on top of the tubes. The points of the cords came through the tiny holes in the points of the tubes, and Almanzo pulled each one tight, and held it tight by sticking a raw potato on the tube's sharp point.

When every tube had its wick, held straight and tight down its middle, Mother carefully poured the hot tallow. She filled every tube to the top. Then Almanzo set the mold outdoors to cool.

When the tallow was hard, he brought the mold in. He pulled off the potatoes. Mother dipped the whole mold quickly into boiling water, and lifted the sticks. Six candles came up on each stick.

Then Almanzo cut them off the stick. He trimmed the ends of wicking off the flat ends, and he left just enough wicking to light, on each pointed end. And he piled the smooth, straight candles in waxy-white piles.

All one day Almanzo helped Mother make candles. That night they had made enough candles to last till butchering-time next year.

Chapter 23

Cobbler

MOTHER was worrying and scolding because the cobbler had not come. Almanzo's moccasins were worn to rags, and Royal had outgrown last year's boots. He had slit them all around, to get his feet into them. Their feet ached with cold, but nothing could be done until the cobbler came.

It was almost time for Royal and Eliza Jane and Alice to go to the Academy, and they had no shoes. And still the cobbler didn't come.

Mother's shears went snickety-snick through

the web of beautiful sheep's-gray cloth she had woven. She cut and fitted and basted and sewed, and she made Royal a handsome new suit, with a greatcoat to match. She made him a cap with flaps that buttoned, like boughten caps.

For Eliza Jane she made a new dress of wine-colored cloth, and she made Alice a new dress of indigo blue. The girls were ripping their old dresses and bonnets, sponging and pressing them and sewing them together again the other side out, to look like new.

In the evenings Mother's knitting-needles flashed and clicked, making new stockings for them all. She knitted so fast that the needles got hot from rubbing together. But they could not have new shoes unless the cobbler came in time.

He didn't come. The girl's skirts hid their old shoes, but Royal had to go to the Academy in his fine suit, with last year's boots that were slit all around and showed his white socks through. It couldn't be helped.

The last morning came. Father and Almanzo did the chores. Every window in the house

blazed with candle-light, and Almanzo missed Royal in the barn.

Royal and the girls were all dressed up at breakfast. No one ate much. Father went to hitch up, and Almanzo lugged the carpet-bags downstairs. He wished Alice wasn't going away.

The sleigh-bells came jingling to the door, and Mother laughed and wiped her eyes with her apron. They all went out to the sleigh. The horses pawed and shook jingles from the bells. Alice tucked the laprobe over her bulging skirts, and Father let the horses go. The sleigh slid by and turned into the road. Alice's black-veiled

287

face looked back and she called,

"Good-by! Good-by!"

Almanzo did not like that day much. Everything seemed large and still and empty. He ate dinner all alone with Father and Mother. Choretime was earlier because Royal was gone. Almanzo hated to go into the house and not see Alice. He even missed Eliza Jane.

After he went to bed he lay awake and wondered what they were doing, five long miles away.

Next morning the cobbler came! Mother went to the door and said to him:

"Well, this is a pretty time to be coming, I must say! Three weeks late, and my children as good as barefoot!"

But the cobbler was so good-natured that she couldn't be angry long. It wasn't his fault; he had been kept three weeks at one house, making shoes for a wedding.

The cobbler was a fat, jolly man. His cheeks and his stomach shook when he chuckled. He set up his cobbler's bench in the dining-room by the window, and opened his box of tools. Already he had Mother laughing at his jokes. Father brought last year's tanned hides, and he and the cobbler discussed them all morning.

Dinner-time was gay. The cobbler told all the news, he praised Mother's cooking, and he told jokes till Father roared and Mother wiped her eyes. Then the cobbler asked Father what he should make first, and Father answered:

"I guess you better begin with boots for Almanzo."

Almanzo could hardly believe it. He had wanted boots for so long. He had thought he must wear moccasins till his feet stopped growing so fast.

"You'll spoil the boy, James," Mother said, but Father answered:

"He's big enough now to wear boots."

Almanzo could hardly wait for the cobbler to begin.

First the cobbler looked at all the wood in the woodshed. He wanted a piece of maple, perfectly seasoned, and with a straight, fine grain.

289

When he found it, he took his small saw, and he sawed off two thin slabs. One was exactly an inch thick; the other was an half inch thick. He measured, and sawed their corners square.

He took the slabs to his cobbler's bench, and sat down, and opened his box of tools. It was divided into little compartments, and every kind of cobbler's tool was neatly laid in them.

The cobbler laid the thicker slab of maplewood on the bench before him. He took a long, sharp knife and cut the whole top of the slab into tiny ridges. Then he turned it around and cut ridges the other way, making tiny, pointed peaks.

He laid the edge of a thin, straight knife in the groove between two ridges, and gently tapped it with a hammer. A thin strip of wood split off, notched all along one side. He moved the knife, and tapped it, till all the wood was in strips. Then holding a strip by one end, he struck his knife in the notches, and every time he struck, a shoe-peg split off. Every peg was an inch long, an eighth of an inch square, and pointed at the end.

The thinner piece of maple he made into pegs, too, and those pegs were half an inch long.

Now the cobbler was ready to measure Almanzo for his boots.

Almanzo took off his moccasins and his socks, and stood on a piece of paper while the cobbler carefully drew around his feet with his big pencil. Then the cobbler measured his feet in every direction, and wrote down the figures.

He did not need Almanzo any more now, so Almanzo helped Father husk corn. He had a little husking-peg, like Father's big one. He buckled the strap around his right mitten, and the wooden peg stood up like a second thumb, between his thumb and fingers.

He and Father sat on milking-stools in the cold barnyard by the corn-shocks. They pulled ears of corn from the stalks; they took the tips of the dry husks between thumb and husking peg, and stripped the husks off the ear of corn.

291

COBBLER

They tossed the bare ears into bushel baskets.

The stalks and rustling long dry leaves they laid in piles. The young stock would eat the leaves.

When they had husked all the corn they could reach, they hitched their stools forward, and slowly worked their way deeper into the tasseled shocks of corn. Husks and stalks piled up behind them. Father emptied the full baskets into the corn-bins, and the bins were filling up.

It was not very cold in the barnyard. The big barns broke the cold winds, and the dry snow shook off the cornstalks. Almanzo's feet were aching, but he thought of his new boots. He could hardly wait till supper-time to see what the cobbler had done.

That day the cobbler had whittled out two wooden lasts, just the shape of Almanzo's feet. They fitted upside-down over a tall peg on his bench, and they would come apart in halves.

Next morning the cobbler cut soles from the thick middle of the cowhide, and inner soles from the thinner leather near the edge. He cut

292

uppers from the softest leather. Then he waxed his thread.

With his right hand he pulled a length of linen thread across the wad of black cobbler's wax in his left palm, and he rolled the thread under his right palm, down the front of his leather apron. Then he pulled it and rolled it again. The wax made a crackling sound, and the cobbler's arms went out and in, out and in, till the thread was shiny-black and stiff with wax.

Then he laid a stiff hog-bristle against each end of it, and he waxed and rolled, waxed and rolled, till the bristles were waxed fast to the thread.

At last he was ready to sew. He laid the upper pieces of one boot together, and clamped them in a vise. The edges stuck up, even and firm. With his awl the cobbler punched a hole through them. He ran the two bristles through the hole, one from each side, and with his strong arms he pulled the thread tight. He bored another hole, ran the two bristles through it,

293

and pulled till the waxed thread sank into the leather. That was one stitch.

"Now that's a seam!" he said. "Your feet won't get damp in my boots, even if you go wading in them. I never sewed a seam yet that wouldn't hold water."

Stitch by stitch he sewed the uppers. When they were done, he laid the soles to soak in water overnight.

Next morning he set one of the lasts on his peg, the sole up. He laid the leather inner-sole on it. He drew the upper part of a boot down over it, folding the edges over the inner sole. Then he laid the heavy sole on top, and there was the boot, upside-down on the last.

The cobbler bored holes with his awl, all around the edge of the sole. Into each hole he drove one of the short maple pegs. He made a heel of thick leather, and pegged it in place with the long maple pegs. The boot was done.

The damp soles had to dry overnight. In the morning the cobbler took out the lasts, and with a rasp he rubbed off the inside ends of the pegs.

Almanzo put on his boots. They fitted perfectly, and the heels thumped grandly on the kitchen floor.

Saturday morning Father drove to Malone to bring home Alice and Royal and Eliza Jane, to be measured for their new shoes. Mother was cooking a big dinner for them, and Almanzo hung around the gate, waiting to see Alice again.

She wasn't a bit changed. Even before she jumped out of the buggy she cried:

"Oh, Almanzo, you've got new boots!" She was studying to be a fine lady; she told Almanzo all about her lessons in music and deportment, but she was glad to be at home again.

Eliza Jane was more bossy than ever. She said Almanzo's boots made too much noise. She even told Mother that she was mortified because Father drank tea from his saucer.

"My land! how else would he cool it?" Mother asked.

"It isn't the style to drink out of saucers any more," Eliza Jane said. "Nice people drink out of the cup."

"Eliza Jane!" Alice cried. "Be ashamed! I guess Father's as nice as anybody!"

Mother actually stopped working. She took her hands out of the dishpan and turned round to face Eliza Jane.

"Young lady," she said, "if you have to show off your fine education, you tell me where saucers come from."

Eliza Jane opened her mouth, and shut it, and looked foolish.

"They come from China," Mother said. "Dutch sailors brought them from China, two hundred years ago, the first time sailors ever sailed around the Cape of Good Hope and found China. Up to that time, folks drank out of cups; they didn't have saucers. Ever since they've had saucers, they've drunk out of them. I guess a thing that folks have done for two hundred years we can keep on doing. We're not likely to change, for a new-fangled notion that you've got in Malone Academy."

That shut up Eliza Jane.

Royal did not say much. He put on old clothes and did his share of the chores, but he did not seem interested. And that night in bed he told Almanzo he was going to be a store-keeper.

"You're a bigger fool than I be, if you drudge all your days on a farm," he said.

"I like horses," said Almanzo.

"Huh! Storekeepers have horses," Royal answered. "They dress up every day, and keep clean, and they ride around with a carriage and pair. There's men in the cities have coachmen to drive them."

Almanzo did not say anything, but he did not want a coachman. He wanted to break colts, and he wanted to drive his own horses, himself.

Next morning they all went to church together. They left Royal and Eliza Jane and Alice at the Academy; only the cobbler came back to the farm. Every day he whistled and worked at his bench in the dining-room, till all the boots and shoes were done. He was there two weeks, and when he loaded his bench and tools in his buggy and drove away to his next customer, the house seemed empty and still again.

That evening Father said to Almanzo,

"Well, son, corn-husking's done. What say we make a bobsled for Star and Bright, tomorrow?"

"Oh, Father!" Almanzo said. "Can I—will you let me haul wood from the timber this winter?"

Father's eyes twinkled. "What else would you need a bobsled for?" he asked.

Chapter 24.

The Little Bobsled

SNOW was falling next morning when Almanzo rode with Father to the timber lot. Large feathery flakes made a veil over everything, and if you were alone and held your breath and listened, you could hear the soft, tiny sound of their falling.

Father and Almanzo tramped through the falling snow in the woods, looking for straight, small oaks. When they found one, Father chopped it down. He chopped off all the limbs,

299

and Almanzo piled them up neatly. Then they loaded the small logs on the bobsled.

After that they looked for two small crooked trees to make curved runners. They must be five inches through, and six feet tall before they began to curve. It was hard to find them. In the whole timber lot there were no two trees alike.

"You wouldn't find two alike in the whole world, son," Father said. "Not even two blades of grass are the same. Everything is different from everything else, if you look at it."

They had to take two trees that were a little alike. Father chopped them down and Almanzo helped load them on the bobsled. Then they drove home, in time for dinner.

That afternoon Father and Almanzo made the little bobsled, on the Big-Barn Floor.

First Father hewed the bottoms of the runners flat and smooth, clear around the crook of their turned-up front ends. Just behind the crook he hewed a flat place on top, and he hewed another flat place near the rear ends.

Then he hewed two beams for cross-pieces.

He hewed them ten inches wide and three inches high, and sawed them four feet long. They were to stand on edge. He hewed out their corners, to fit over the flat places on top of the runners. Then he hewed out a curve in their underneath edges, to let them slip over the high snow in the middle of the road.

He laid the runners side by side, three and a half feet apart, and he fitted the cross-beams on them. But he did not fasten them together yet.

He hewed out two slabs, six feet long and flat on both sides. He laid them on the cross-beams, over the runners.

Then with an auger he bored a hole through a slab, down past the cross-beam, into the runner. He bored close to the beam, and the auger made half an auger-hole down the side of the beam. On the other side of the beam he bored another hole like the first.

Into the holes he drove stout wooden pegs. The pegs went down through the slab and into the runner, and they fitted tightly into the half-holes on both sides of the beam. Two pegs held the slab and the beam and the runner firmly together, at one corner of the sled.

In the other three corners he bored the holes, and Almanzo hammered in the pegs. That finished the body of the little bobsled.

Now Father bored a hole cross-wise in each runner, close to the front cross-beam. He hewed the bark from a slender pole, and sharpened its ends so that they would go into the holes.

Almanzo and Father pulled the curved ends of the runners as far apart as they could, and Father slipped the ends of the pole into the holes. When Almanzo and Father let go, the runners held the pole firmly between them.

Then Father bored two holes in the pole, close to the runners. They were to hold the sled's tongue. For the tongue he used an elm sapling, because elm is tougher and more pliable than oak. The sapling was ten feet long from butt to tip. Father slipped an iron ring over the tip and hammered it down till it fitted tightly, two feet and a half from the butt. He split the butt in two, up to the iron ring, which kept it from splitting any farther.

He sharpened the split ends and spread them apart, and drove them into the holes in the cross-wise pole. Then he bored holes down through the pole into the two ends of the tongue, and drove pegs into the holes.

Near the tip of the tongue he drove an iron spike down through it. The spike stuck out below the tongue. The tip of the tongue would

go into the iron ring in the bottom of the calves' yoke, and when they backed, the ring would push against the spike, and the stiff tongue would push the sled backward.

Now the bobsled was done. It was almost chore-time, but Almanzo did not want to leave his little bobsled until it had a wood-rack. So Father quickly bored holes down through the ends of the slabs into the cross-beams, and into each hole Almanzo drove a stake four feet long. The tall stakes stood up at the corners of the sled. They would hold the logs when he hauled wood from the timber.

The storm was rising. The falling snow whirled and the wind was crying with a lonely sound when Almanzo and Father carried the full milk-pails to the house that night.

Almanzo wanted deep snow, so that he could begin hauling wood with the new sled. But Father listened to the storm, and said that they could not work outdoors next day. They would have to stay under shelter, so they might as well begin threshing the wheat.

Chapter 25

Threshing

T H E wind howled and the snow whirled and a mournful sound came from the cedars. The skeleton apple trees rattled their branches together like bones. All outdoors was dark and wild and noisy.

But the solid, strong barns were quiet. The howling storm beat upon them, but the barns stood undisturbed. They kept their own warmth inside themselves.

When Almanzo latched the door behind him, the noise of the storm was not so loud as the

305

warm stillness of the barns. The air was quiet. The horses turned in their box-stalls and whinnied softly; the colts tossed their heads and pawed. The cows stood in a row, placidly swinging their tasseled tails; you could hear them chewing their cuds.

Almanzo stroked the soft noses of the horses, and looked longingly at the bright-eyed colts. Then he went to the toolshed where Father was mending a flail.

The flail had come off its handle and Father had put them together again. The flail was an ironwood stick, three feet long and as big around as a broom-handle. It had a hole through one end. Its handle was five feet long, and one end was a round knob.

Father put a strip of cowhide through the hole in the flail, and riveted the ends together to make a leather loop. He took another strip of cowhide and cut a slit in each end of it. He put it through the leather loop on the flail, then he pushed the slits over the knobbed end of the handle.

The flail and its handle were loosely held together by the two leather loops, and the flail could swing easily in any direction.

Almanzo's flail was just like Father's, but it was new and did not need mending. When Father's flail was ready, they went to the South-Barn Floor.

There was still a faint smell of pumpkins, though the stock had eaten them all. A woodsy smell came from the pile of beech leaves, and a dry, strawy smell came from the wheat. Outside the wind was screeching and the snow was whirling, but the South-Barn Floor was warm and quiet.

Father and Almanzo unbound several sheaves of wheat and spread them on the clean wooden floor.

Almanzo asked Father why he did not hire the machine that did threshing. Three men had brought it into the country last fall, and Father had gone to see it. It would thresh a man's whole grain crop in a few days.

"That's a lazy man's way to thresh," Father

said. "Haste makes waste, but a lazy man'd rather get his work done fast than do it himself. That machine chews up the straw till it's not fit to feed stock, and it scatters grain around and wastes it.

"All it saves is time, son. And what good is time, with nothing to do? You want to sit and twiddle your thumbs, all these stormy winter days?"

"No!" said Almanzo. He had enough of that, on Sundays.

They spread the wheat two or three inches thick on the floor. Then they faced each other, and they took the handles of their flails in both hands; they swung the flails above their heads and brought them down on the wheat.

Father's struck, then Almanzo's; then Father's, then Almanzo's. THUD! Thud! THUD! Thud! It was like marching to the music on Independence Day. It was like beating the drum. THUD! Thud! THUD! Thud!

The grains of wheat were shelling from their little husks and sifting down through the straw.

308

A faint, good smell came from the beaten straw, like the smell of the ripe fields in the sun.

Before Almanzo tired of swinging the flail, it was time to use the pitchforks. He lifted the straw lightly, shaking it, then pitched it aside. The brown wheat-grains lay scattered on the floor. Almanzo and Father spread more sheaves over it, then took up their flails again.

When the shelled grain was thick on the floor, Almanzo scraped it aside with a big wooden scraper.

All that day the pile of wheat grew higher. Just before chore-time Almanzo swept the floor in front of the fanning-mill. Then Father shoveled wheat into the hopper, while Almanzo turned the fanning-mill's handle.

The fans whirred inside the mill, a cloud of chaff blew out its front, and the kernels of clean wheat poured out of its side and went sliding down the rising heap on the floor. Almanzo put a handful into his mouth; they were sweet to chew, and lasted a long time.

He chewed while he held the grain-sacks and

Father shoveled the wheat into them. Father stood the full sacks in a row against the wall— a good day's work had been done.

"What say we run some beechnuts through?" Father asked. So they pitched beech leaves into the hopper, and now the whirring fans blew away the leaves, and the three-cornered brown nuts poured out. Almanzo filled a peck-measure with them, to eat that evening by the heater.

Then he went whistling to do the chores.

All winter long, on stormy days, there would be threshing to do. When the wheat was threshed, there would be the oats, the beans, the Canada peas. There was plenty of grain to feed the stock, plenty of wheat and rye to take to the mill for flour. Almanzo had harrowed the fields, he had helped in the harvest, and now he was threshing.

He helped to feed the patient cows, and the horses eagerly whinnying over the bars of their stalls, and the hungrily bleating sheep, and the grunting pigs. And he felt like saying to them all:

310

"You can depend on me. I'm big enough to take care of you all."

Then he shut the door snugly behind him, leaving them all fed and warm and comfortable for the night, and he went trudging through the storm to the good supper waiting in the kitchen.

Chapter 26

Christmas

FOR A long time it seemed that Christmas would never come. On Christmas, Uncle Andrew and Aunt Delia, Uncle Wesley and Aunt Lindy, and all the cousins were coming to dinner. It would be the best dinner of the whole year. And a good boy might get something in his stocking. Bad boys found nothing but switches in their stockings on Christmas morning. Almanzo tried to be good for so long that he could hardly stand the strain.

But at last it was the day before Christmas, and Alice and Royal and Eliza Jane were home again. The girls were cleaning the whole house, and Mother was baking. Royal could help Father with the threshing, but Almanzo had to help in the house. He remembered the switch, and tried to be willing and cheerful.

He had to scour the steel knives and forks, and polish the silver. He had to wear an apron round his neck. He took the scouring-brick and scraped a pile of red dust off it, and then with a wet cloth he rubbed the dust up and down on the knives and forks.

The kitchen was full of delicious smells. Newly baked bread was cooling, frosted cakes and cookies and mince pies and pumpkin pies filled the pantry shelves, cranberries bubbled on the stove. Mother was making dressing for the goose.

Outdoors, the sun was shining on the snow. The icicles twinkled all along the eaves. Far away sleigh-bells faintly jingled, and from the barns came the joyful thud-thud! thud-thud!

of the flails. But when all the steel knives and forks were done, Almanzo soberly polished the silver.

Then he had to run to the attic for sage; he had to run down cellar for apples, and upstairs again for onions. He filled the woodbox. He hurried in the cold to fetch water from the pump. He thought maybe he was through, then, anyway for a minute. But no; he had to polish the dining-room side of the stove.

"Do the parlor side yourself, Eliza Jane," Mother said. "Almanzo might spill the blacking."

Almanzo's insides quaked. He knew what would happen if Mother knew about that black splotch, hidden on the parlor wall. He didn't want to get a switch in his Christmas stocking, but he would far rather find a switch there than have Father take him to the woodshed.

That night everyone was tired, and the house was so clean and neat that nobody dared touch anything. After supper Mother put the stuffed, fat goose and the little pig into the heater's oven to roast slowly all night. Father set the dampers and wound the clock. Almanzo and Royal hung clean socks on the back of a chair, and Alice and Eliza Jane hung stockings on the back of another chair.

Then they all took candles and went to bed.

It was still dark when Almanzo woke up. He felt excited, and then he remembered that this was Christmas morning. He jerked back the covers and jumped onto something alive that squirmed. It was Royal. He had forgotten that Royal was there, but he scrambled over him, yelling:

"Christmas! Christmas! Merry Christmas!"

He pulled his trousers over his nightshirt. Royal jumped out of bed and lighted the candle. Almanzo grabbed the candle, and Royal shouted:

"Hi! Leave that be! Where's my pants?"

But Almanzo was already running downstairs. Alice and Eliza Jane were flying from their room, but Almanzo beat them. He saw his sock hanging all lumpy; he set down the

315

candle and grabbed his sock. The first thing he pulled out was a cap, a boughten cap!

The plaid cloth was machine-woven. So was the lining. Even the sewing was machine-sewing. And the ear-muffs were buttoned over the top.

Almanzo yelled. He had not even hoped for such a cap. He looked at it, inside and out; he felt the cloth and the sleek lining. He put the cap on his head. It was a little large, because he was growing. So he could wear it a long time.

Eliza Jane and Alice were digging into their stockings and squealing, and Royal had a silk muffler. Almanzo thrust his hand into his sock again, and pulled out a nickel's worth of hore-hound candy. He bit off the end of one stick. The outside melted like maple sugar, but the inside was hard and could be sucked for hours.

Then he pulled out a new pair of mittens. Mother had knit the wrists and backs in a fancy stitch. He pulled out an orange, and he pulled out a little package of dried figs. And he thought that was all. He thought no boy ever had a better Christmas.

But in the toe of the sock there was still something more. It was small and thin and hard. Almanzo couldn't imagine what it was. He pulled it out, and it was a jack-knife. It had four blades.

Almanzo yelled and yelled. He snapped all the blades open, sharp and shining, and he yelled,

"Alice, look! Look, Royal! Lookee, lookee my jack-knife! Looky my cap!"

Father's voice came out of the dark bedroom and said:

"Look at the clock."

They all looked at one another. Then Royal held up the candle and they looked at the tall clock. Its hands pointed to half past three.

Even Eliza Jane did not know what to do. They had waked up Father and Mother, an hour and a half before time to get up.

"What time is it?" Father asked.

Almanzo looked at Royal. Royal and Almanzo looked at Eliza Jane. Eliza Jane swallowed, and opened her mouth, but Alice said:

"Merry Christmas, Father! Merry Christ-

317

mas, Mother! It's—it's—thirty minutes to four, Father."

The clock said, "Tick! Tock! Tick! Tock! Tick!" Then Father chuckled.

Royal opened the dampers of the heater, and Eliza Jane stirred up the kitchen fire and put the kettle on. The house was warm and cosy when Father and Mother got up, and they had a whole hour to spare. There was time to enjoy the presents.

Alice had a gold locket, and Eliza Jane had a pair of garnet earrings. Mother had knitted new lace collars and black lace mitts for them both. Royal had the silk muffler and a fine leather wallet. But Almanzo thought he had the best presents of all. It was a wonderful Christmas.

Then Mother began to hurry, and to hurry everyone else. There were the chores to do, the milk to skim, the new milk to strain and put away, breakfast to eat, vegetables to be peeled, and the whole house must be put in order and everybody dressed up before the company came.

318

The sun rushed up the sky. Mother was everywhere, talking all the time. "Almanzo, wash your ears! Goodness mercy, Royal, don't stand around underfoot! Eliza Jane, remember you're paring those potatoes, not slicing them, and don't leave so many eyes they can see to jump out of the pot. Count the silver, Alice, and piece it out with the steel knives and forks. The best bleached tablecloths are on the bottom shelf. Mercy on us, look at that clock!"

Sleigh-bells came jingling up the road, and Mother slammed the oven door and ran to change her apron and pin on her brooch; Alice ran downstairs and Eliza Jane ran upstairs, both of them told Almanzo to straighten his collar. Father was calling Mother to fold his cravat. Then Uncle Wesley's sleigh stopped with a last clash of bells.

Almanzo ran out, whooping, and Father and Mother came behind him, as calm as if they had never hurried in their lives. Frank and Fred and Abner and Mary tumbled out of the sleigh, all bundled up, and before Aunt Lindy had handed

Mother the baby, Uncle Andrew's sleigh was coming. The yard was full of boys and the house filled with hoopskirts. The uncles stamped snow off their boots and unwound their mufflers.

Royal and Cousin James drove the sleighs into the buggy-house; they unhitched the horses and put them in stalls and rubbed down their snowy legs.

Almanzo was wearing his boughten cap, and he showed the cousins his jack-knife. Frank's cap was old now. He had a jack-knife, but it had only three blades.

Then Almanzo showed his cousins Star and Bright, and the little bobsled, and he let them scratch Lucy's fat white back with corncobs. He said they could look at Starlight if they'd be quiet and not scare him.

The beautiful colt twitched his tail, and came daintily stepping toward them. Then he tossed his head and shied away from Frank's hand thrust through the bars.

"You leave him be!" Almanzo said.

"I bet you don't dast go in there and get on his back," said Frank.

"I dast, but I got better sense," Almanzo told him. "I know better than to spoil that fine colt."

"How'd it spoil him?" Frank said. "Yah, you're scared he'd hurt you! You're scared of that little bitty colt!"

"I am not scared," said Almanzo. "But Father won't let me."

"I guess I'd do it if I wanted to, if I was you. I guess your father wouldn't know," Frank said.

Almanzo didn't answer, and Frank got up on the bars of the stall.

"You get down off there!" Almanzo said, and he took hold of Frank's leg. "Don't you scare that colt!"

"I'll scare him if I want to," Frank said, kicking. Almanzo hung on. Starlight was running around and around the stall, and Almanzo wanted to yell for Royal. But he knew that would frighten Starlight even more.

He set his teeth and gave a mighty tug, and Frank came tumbling down. All the horses jumped, and Starlight reared and smashed against the manger.

"I'll lick you for that," Frank said, scrambling up.

"You just try to lick me!" said Almanzo.

Royal came hurrying from the South Barn. He took Almanzo and Frank by the shoulders and marched them outdoors. Fred and Abner and John came silently after them, and Al-

manzo's knees wabbled. He was afraid Royal would tell Father.

"Let me catch you boys fooling around those colts again," Royal said, "and I'll tell Father and Uncle Wesley. You'll get the hides thrashed off you."

Royal shook Almanzo so hard that he couldn't tell how hard Royal was shaking Frank. Then he knocked their heads together. Almanzo saw stars.

"Let that teach you to fight. On Christmas Day! For shame!" Royal said.

"I only didn't want him to scare Starlight," Almanzo said.

"Shut up!" said Royal. "Don't be a tattle-tale. Now you behave yourselves or you'll wish you had. Go wash your hands; it's dinner-time."

They all went into the kitchen and washed their hands. Mother and the aunts and the girl cousins were taking up the Christmas dinner. The dining-table had been turned around and pulled out till it was almost as long as the dining-room, and every inch of it was loaded with good things to eat.

Almanzo bowed his head and shut his eyes tight while Father said the blessing. It was a long blessing, because this was Christmas Day. But at last Almanzo could open his eyes. He sat and silently looked at that table.

He looked at the crisp, crackling little pig lying on the blue platter with an apple in its mouth. He looked at the fat roast goose, the drumsticks sticking up, and the edges of dressing curling out. The sound of Father's knife sharpening on the whetstone made him even hungrier.

He looked at the big bowl of cranberry jelly, and at the fluffy mountain of mashed potatoes with melting butter trickling down it. He looked at the heap of mashed turnips, and the golden baked squash, and the pale fried parsnips.

He swallowed hard and tried not to look any more. He couldn't help seeing the fried apples-'n'onions, and the candied carrots. He couldn't help gazing at the triangles of pie, waiting by his plate; the spicy pumpkin pie, the melting cream pie, the rich, dark mince oozing from between the mince pie's flaky crusts.

He squeezed his hands together between his knees. He had to sit silent and wait, but he felt aching and hollow inside.

All grown-ups at the head of the table must be served first. They were passing their plates, and talking, and heartlessly laughing. The tender pork fell away in slices under Father's carving-knife. The white breast of the goose went piece by piece from the bare breast-bone. Spoons ate up the clear cranberry jelly, and gouged deep into the mashed potatoes, and ladled away the brown gravies.

Almanzo had to wait to the very last. He was youngest of all, except Abner and the babies, and Abner was company.

At last Almanzo's plate was filled. The first taste made a pleasant feeling inside him, and it grew and grew, while he ate and ate and ate. He ate till he could eat no more, and he felt very good inside. For a while he slowly nibbled bits from his second piece of fruitcake. Then he put the fruity slice in his pocket and went out to play.

Royal and James were choosing sides, to play

snow-fort. Royal chose Frank, and James chose Almanzo. When everyone was chosen, they all went to work, rolling snowballs through the deep drifts by the barn. They rolled till the balls were almost as tall as Almanzo; then they rolled them into a wall. They packed snow between them, and made a good fort.

Then each side made its own little snowballs. They breathed on the snow, and squeezed it solid. They made dozens of hard snowballs. When they were ready for the fight, Royal threw a stick into the air and caught it when it came down. James took hold of the stick above Royal's hand, then Royal took hold of it above James' hand, and so on to the end of the stick. James' hand was last, so James' side had the fort.

How the snowballs flew! Almanzo ducked and dodged and yelled, and threw snowballs as fast as he could, till they were all gone. Royal came charging over the wall with all the enemy after him, and Almanzo rose up and grabbed Frank. Headlong they went into the deep snow, outside the wall, and they rolled over and over, hitting each other as hard as they could.

Almanzo's face was covered with snow and his mouth was full of it, but he hung on to Frank and kept hitting at him. Frank got him down, but Almanzo squirmed out from under. Frank's head hit his nose, and it began to bleed. Almanzo didn't care. He was on top of Frank, hitting him as hard as he could in the deep snow. He kept saying, "Holler 'nuff! holler 'nuff!"

Frank grunted and squirmed. He rolled half over, and Almanzo got on top of him. He couldn't stay on top of Frank and hit him, so he bore down with all his weight, and he pushed Frank's face deeper and deeper into the snow. And Frank gasped: "'Nuff!"

Almanzo got up on his knees, and he saw Mother in the doorway of the house. She called,

"Boys! Boys! Stop playing now. It's time to come in and warm."

They were warm. They were hot and panting. But Mother and the aunts thought the cousins must get warm before they rode home in the cold. They all went tramping in, covered with snow, and Mother held up her hands and exclaimed:

"Mercy on us!"

The grown-ups were in the parlor, but the boys had to stay in the dining-room, so they wouldn't melt on the parlor carpet. They couldn't sit down, because the chairs were covered with blankets and laprobes, warming by the heater. But they ate apples and drank cider, standing around, and Almanzo and Abner went into the pantry and ate bits off the platters.

Then uncles and aunts and the girl cousins put on their wraps, and they brought the sleeping babies from the bedroom, rolled up in shawls. The sleighs came jingling from the barn, and Father and Mother helped tuck in the blankets and laprobes, over the hoopskirts. Everybody called: "Good-by! Good-by!"

The music of the sleigh-bells came back for a little while; then it was gone. Christmas was over.

Chapter 27

Wood-Hauling

W H E N school opened as usual, that January, Almanzo did not have to go. He was hauling wood from the timber.

In the frosty cold mornings before the sun was up, Father hitched the big oxen to the big bobsled and Almanzo hitched the yearlings to his bobsled. Star and Bright were now too big for the little yoke, and the larger yoke was too heavy for Almanzo to handle alone. Pierre had to help him lift it onto Star's neck, and Louis helped him push Bright under the other end of it.

The yearlings had been idle all summer in the pastures, and now they did not like to work. They shook their heads and pulled and backed. It was hard to get the bows in place and put the bow-pins in.

Almanzo had to be patient and gentle. He petted the yearlings (when sometimes he wanted to hit them) and he fed them carrots and talked to them soothingly. But before he could get them yoked and hitched to his sled, Father was already going to the timber lot.

Almanzo followed. The yearlings obeyed him when he shouted "Giddap!" and they turned to the right or the left when he cracked his whip and shouted "Gee!" or "Haw!" They trudged along the road, up the hills and down the hills, and Almanzo rode on his bobsled with Pierre and Louis behind him.

He was ten years old now, and he was driving his own oxen on his own sled, and going to the timber to haul wood.

In the woods the snow was drifted high against the trees. The lowest branches of pines and cedars were buried in it. There was no road; there were no marks on the snow but the feather-stitching tracks of birds and the blurry spots where rabbits had hopped. Deep in the still woods axes were chopping with a ringing sound.

Father's big oxen wallowed on, breaking a road, and Almanzo's yearlings struggled behind them. Farther and farther into the woods they went, till they came to the clearing where French Joe and Lazy John were chopping down the trees.

Logs lay all around, half buried in snow. John and Joe had sawed them into fifteen-foot lengths, and some of them were two feet through. The huge logs were so heavy that six men couldn't lift them, but Father had to load them on the bobsled.

He stopped the sled beside one of them, and John and Joe came to help him. They had three stout poles, called skids. They stuck these under the log, and let them slant up to the bobsled. Then they took their cant-poles. Cant-poles have sharp ends, with big iron hooks swinging loose under them.

John and Joe stood near the ends of the log. They put the sharp ends of their cant-poles against it, and when they raised the poles up, the cant-hooks bit into the log and rolled it a little. Then Father caught hold of the middle of the log with his cant-pole and hook, and he held it from rolling back, while John and Joe quickly let their cant-hooks slip down and take another bite. They rolled the log a little more, and again Father held it, and again they rolled it.

They rolled the log little by little, up the slanting skids and onto the bobsled.

But Almanzo had no cant-hooks, and he had to load his sled.

He found three straight poles to use for skids. Then with shorter poles he started to load some of the smallest logs. They were eight or nine inches through and about ten feet long and they were crooked and hard to handle.

Almanzo put Pierre and Louis near the ends of a log and he stood in the middle, like Father. They pushed and pried and lifted and gasped, pushing the log up the skids. It was hard to do, because their poles had no cant-hooks and could not take hold of the log.

They managed to load six logs; then they had

to put more logs on top of those, and this made the skids slant upward more steeply. Father's bobsled was loaded already, and Almanzo hurried. He cracked his whip and urged Star and Bright quickly to the nearest log.

One end of this log was bigger than the other, so it would not roll evenly. Almanzo put Louis at the smaller end, and told him not to roll it too fast. Pierre and Louis rolled the log an inch, then Almanzo stuck his pole under it and held it, while Pierre and Louis rolled it again. They got the log high up on the steep skids.

Almanzo was holding it up with all his might. His legs were braced and his teeth were clenched and his neck strained and his eyes felt bulging out, when suddenly the whole log slipped.

The pole jerked out of his hands and hit his head. The log was falling on him. He tried to get away, but it smashed him down into the snow.

Pierre and Louis screamed and kept screaming. Almanzo couldn't get up. The log was on top of him. Father and John lifted it, and Almanzo crawled out. He managed to get up on his feet.

"Hurt, son?" Father asked him.

Almanzo was afraid he was going to be sick at his stomach. He managed to say, "No, Father."

Father felt his shoulders and arms.

"Well, well, no bones broken!" Father said cheerfully.

"Lucky the snow's deep," said John. "Or he might have been hurt bad."

"Accidents will happen, son," Father said. "Take more care next time. Men must look out for themselves in the timber."

Almanzo wanted to lie down. His head hurt and his stomach hurt and his right foot hurt dreadfully. But he helped Pierre and Louis straighten the log, and he did not try to hurry this time. They got the log on the sled all right, but not before Father was gone with his load.

Almanzo decided not to load any more logs now. He climbed onto the load and cracked his whip and shouted:

335

"Giddap!"

Star and Bright pulled, but the sled did not move. Then Star tried to pull, and quit trying. Bright tried, and gave up just as Star tried again. They both stopped, discouraged.

"Giddap! Giddap!" Almanzo kept shouting, cracking his whip.

Star tried again, then Bright, then Star. The sled did not move. Star and Bright stood still, puffing out the breath from their noses. Almanzo felt like crying and swearing. He shouted:

"Giddap! Giddap!"

John and Joe stopped sawing, and Joe came over to the sled.

"You're too heavy loaded," he said. "You boys get down and walk. And Almanzo, you talk to your team and gentle them along. You'll make them steers balky if you don't be careful."

Almanzo climbed down. He rubbed the yearlings' throats and scratched around their horns. He lifted the yoke a little and ran his hand under it, then settled it gently in place. All the time he talked to the little steers. Then

336

he stood beside Star and cracked his whip and shouted:

"Giddap!"

Star and Bright pulled together, and the sled moved.

Almanzo trudged all the way home. Pierre and Louis walked in the smooth tracks behind the runners, but Almanzo had to struggle through the soft, deep snow beside Star.

When he reached the woodpile at home, Father said he had done well to get out of the timber.

"Next time, son, you'll know better than to put on such a heavy load before the road's broken," Father said. "You spoil a team if you let them see-saw. They get the idea they can't pull the load, and they quit trying. After that, they're no good.

Almanzo could not eat dinner. He felt sick, and his foot ached. Mother thought perhaps he should stop work, but Almanzo would not let a little accident stop him.

Still, he was slow. Before he reached the timber he met Father coming back with a load. He knew that an empty sled must always give the road to a loaded sled, so he cracked his whip and shouted:

"Gee!"

Star and Bright swerved to the right, and before Almanzo could even yell they were sinking in the deep snow in the ditch. They did not know how to break road, like big oxen. They snorted and floundered and plunged, and the sled was sinking under the snow. The little steers tried to turn around; the twisted yoke was almost choking them.

Almanzo struggled in the snow, trying to reach the yearlings' heads. Father turned and watched, while he went by. Then he faced forward again and drove on toward home.

Almanzo got hold of Star's head and spoke to him gently. Pierre and Louis had hold of Bright, and the yearlings stopped plunging. Only their heads and their backs showed above the snow. Almanzo swore:

"Gol ding it!"

They had to dig out the steers and the sled. They had no shovel. They had to move all that snow with their hands and feet. There was nothing else they could do.

It took them a long time. But they kicked and pawed all the snow away from in front of the sled and the steers. They tramped it hard and smooth in front of the runners. Almanzo straightened the tongue and the chain and the yoke.

He had to sit down and rest a minute. But he got up, and he petted Star and Bright and spoke to them encouragingly. He took an apple away from Pierre and broke it in two and gave it to the little steers. When they had eaten it, he cracked his whip and cheerfully shouted:

"Giddap!"

Pierre and Louis pushed the sled with all their might. The sled started. Almanzo shouted and cracked his whip. Star and Bright hunched their backs and pulled. Up they went out of the ditch, and up went the sled with a lurch.

That was one trouble Almanzo had got out of, all by himself.

The road in the woods was fairly well broken now, and this time Almanzo did not put so many logs on the sled. So he rode homeward on the load, with Pierre and Louis sitting behind him.

Down the long road he saw Father coming, and he said to himself that this time Father must turn out to let him go by.

Star and Bright walked briskly and the sled was sliding easily down the white road. Almanzo's whip cracked loudly in the frosty air. Nearer and nearer came Father's big oxen, and Father riding on the big sled.

Now of course the big oxen should have made way for Almanzo's load. But perhaps Star and Bright remembered that they had turned out before. Or perhaps they knew they must be polite to older, bigger oxen. Nobody expected them to turn out of the road, but suddenly they did.

One sled-runner dropped into soft snow. And over went the sled and the load and the boys, topsy-turvy, pell-mell.

Almanzo went sprawling through the air and headfirst into snow.

He wallowed and scrambled and came up. His sled stood on edge. The logs were scattered and up-ended in the drifts. There was a pile of red-brown legs and sides deep in the snow. Father's big oxen were going calmly by.

Pierre and Louis rose out of the snow, swearing in French. Father stopped his oxen and got off his sled.

"Well, well, well, son," he said. "Seems we've met again."

Almanzo and Father looked at the yearlings. Bright lay on Star; their legs and the chain and the tongue were all mixed up, and the yoke was over Star's ears. The yearlings lay still, too sensible to try to move. Father helped untangle them and get them on their feet. They were not hurt.

Father helped set Almanzo's sled on its runners. With his sled-stakes for skids, and Almanzo's sled-stakes for poles, he loaded the logs again. Then he stood back and said nothing

341

while Almanzo yoked up Star and Bright, and petted and encouraged them, and made them haul the tilted load along the edge of the ditch and safely into the road.

"That's the way, son!" Father said, "Down again, up again!"

He drove on to the timber, and Almanzo drove on to the woodpile at home.

All that week and all the next week he went on hauling wood from the timber. He was learning to be a pretty good ox-driver and wood-hauler. Every day his foot ached a little less, and at last he hardly limped at all.

He helped Father haul a huge pile of logs, ready to be sawed and split and corded in the woodshed.

Then one evening Father said they had hauled that year's supply of wood, and Mother said it was high time Almanzo went to school, if he was going to get any schooling that winter.

Almanzo said there was threshing to do, and the young calves needed breaking. He asked:

"What do I have to go to school for? I can

342

read and write and spell, and I don't want to be a school-teacher or a storekeeper."

"You can read and write and spell," Father said, slowly. "But can you figure?"

"Yes, Father," Almanzo said. "Yes, I can figure—some."

"A farmer must know more figuring than that, son. You better go to school."

Almanzo did not say any more; he knew it would be no use. Next morning he took his dinner-pail and went to school.

This year his seat was farther back in the room, so he had a desk for his books and slate. And he studied hard to learn the whole arithmetic, because the sooner he knew it all, the sooner he would not have to go to school any more.

Chapter 28

Mr. Thompson's Pocketbook

FATHER had so much hay that year that the stock could not eat it all, so he decided to sell some of it in town. He went to the woods and brought back a straight, smooth ash log. He hewed the bark from it, and then with a wooden maul he beat the log, turning it and pounding it until he softened the layer of wood that had grown last summer, and loosened the thin layer of wood underneath it, which had grown the summer before.

Then with his knife he cut long gashes from end to end of the log, about an inch and a half apart. And he peeled off that thin, tough layer of wood in strips about an inch and a half wide. Those were ash withes.

When Almanzo saw them piled on the Big-Barn Floor, he guessed that Father was going to bale hay, and he asked:

"Be you going to need help?"

Father's eyes twinkled. "Yes, son," he said. "You can stay home from school. You won't learn hay-baling any younger."

Early next morning Mr. Weed, the hay-baler, came with his press and Almanzo helped to set it up on the Big-Barn Floor. It was a stout wooden box, as long and wide as a bale of hay, but ten feet high. Its cover could be fastened on tightly, and its bottom was loose. Two iron levers were hinged to the loose bottom, and the levers ran on little wheels on iron tracks going out from each end of the box.

The tracks were like small railroad tracks, and the press was called a railroad press. It was a new, fine machine for baling hay.

In the barnyard Father and Mr. Webb set up a capstan, with a long sweep on it. A rope from the capstan went through a ring under the hay-press, and was tied to another rope that went to the wheels at the end of the levers.

When everything was ready, Almanzo hitched Bess to the sweep. Father pitched hay into the box, and Mr. Weed stood in the box and trampled it down, till the box would hold no more. Then he fastened the cover on the box, and Father called,

"All right, Almanzo!"

Almanzo slapped Bess with the lines and shouted,

"Giddap, Bess!"

Bess began to walk around the capstan, and the capstan began to wind up the rope. The rope pulled the ends of the levers toward the press, and the inner ends of the levers pushed its loose bottom upward. The bottom slowly rose, squeezing the hay. The rope creaked and the box groaned, till the hay was pressed so tight

346

it couldn't be pressed tighter. Then Father shouted, "Whoa!" And Almanzo shouted, "Whoa, Bess!"

Father climbed up the hay-press and ran ash withes through narrow cracks in the box. He pulled them tight around the bale of hay, and knotted them firmly.

Mr. Weed unfastened the cover, and up popped the bale of hay, bulging between the tight ash-withes. It weighed 250 pounds, but Father lifted it easily.

Then Father and Mr. Weed re-set the press, Almanzo unwound the rope from the capstan, and they began again to make another bale of hay. All day they worked, and that night Father said they had baled enough.

Almanzo sat at the supper table, wishing he did not have to go back to school. He thought about figuring, and he was thinking so hard that words came out of his mouth before he knew it.

"Thirty bales to a load, at two dollars a bale," he said. "That's sixty dollars a lo——"

He stopped, scared. He knew better than to

347

speak at table, when he wasn't spoken to.

"Mercy on us, listen to the boy!" Mother said.

"Well, well, son!" said Father. "I see you've been studying to some purpose." He drank the tea out of his saucer, set it down, and looked again at Almanzo. "Learning is best put into practice. What say you ride to town with me tomorrow, and sell that load of hay?"

"Oh yes! Please, Father!" Almanzo almost shouted.

He did not have to go to school next morning. He climbed high up on top of the load of hay, and lay there on his stomach and kicked up his heels. Father's hat was down below him, and beyond were the plump backs of the horses. He was as high up as if he were in a tree.

The load swayed a little, and the wagon creaked, and the horses' feet made dull sounds on the hard snow. The air was clear and cold, the sky was very blue, and all the snowy fields were sparkling.

Just beyond the bridge over Trout River, Almanzo saw a small black thing lying beside the road. When the wagon passed, he leaned over the edge of the hay and saw that it was a pocketbook. He yelled, and Father stopped the horses to let him climb down and pick it up. It was a fat, black wallet.

Almanzo shinnied up the bales of hay and the horses went on. He looked at the pocketbook. He opened it, and it was full of banknotes. There was nothing to show who owned them.

He handed it down to Father, and Father gave him the reins. The team seemed far below, with the lines slanting down to the hames, and Almanzo felt very small. But he liked to drive. He held the lines carefully and the horses went steadily along. Father was looking at the pocketbook and the money.

"There's fifteen hundred dollars here," Father said. "Now who does it belong to? He's a man who's afraid of banks, or he wouldn't carry so much money around. You can see by the creases in the bills, he's carried them some time. They're big bills, and folded together, so likely he got them all at once. Now who's suspicious, and stingy, and sold something valuable lately?"

Almanzo didn't know, but Father didn't expect him to answer. The horses went around a curve in the road as well as if Father had been driving them.

"Thompson!" Father exclaimed. "He sold some land last fall. He's afraid of banks, and he's suspicious, and so stingy he'd skin a flea for its hide and tallow. Thompson's the man!"

He put the pocketbook in his pocket and took the lines from Almanzo. "We'll see if we can find him in town," he said.

Father drove first to the Livery, Sale and Feed Stable. The liveryman came out, and sure enough Father let Almanzo sell the hay. He stood back and did not say anything, while Almanzo showed the liveryman that the hay was good timothy and clover, clean and bright, and every bale solid and full weight.

"How much do you want for it?" the liveryman asked.

"Two dollars and a quarter a bale," Almanzo said.

"I won't pay that price," said the liveryman. "It isn't worth it."

"What would you call a fair price?" Almanzo asked him.

"Not a penny over two dollars," the liveryman said.

"All right, I'll take two dollars," said Almanzo, quickly.

The liveryman looked at Father, and then he pushed back his hat and asked Almanzo why he priced the hay at two dollars and a quarter in the first place.

"Are you taking it at two dollars?" Almanzo asked. The liveryman said he was. "Well," Almanzo said, "I asked two and a quarter because if I'd asked two, you wouldn't have paid but one seventy-five."

The liveryman laughed, and said to Father, "That's a smart boy of yours."

"Time will show," Father said. "Many a good beginning makes a bad ending. It remains to be seen how he turns out in the long run."

Father did not take the money for the hay;

351

he let Almanzo take it and count it to make sure it was sixty dollars.

Then they went to Mr. Case's store. This store was always crowded, but Father always did his trading there, because Mr. Case sold his goods cheaper than other merchants. Mr. Case said, "I'd rather have a nimble sixpence than a slow shilling."

Almanzo stood in the crowd with Father, waiting while Mr. Case served first-comers. Mr. Case was polite and friendly to everybody alike; he had to be, because they were all customers. Father was polite to everybody, too, but he was not as friendly to some as he was to others.

After a while Father gave Almanzo the pocketbook and told him to look for Mr. Thompson. Father must stay in the store to wait his turn; he could not lose time if they were to get home by chore-time.

No other boys were on the street; they were all in school. Almanzo liked to be walking down the street, carrying all that money, and he

352

thought how glad Mr. Thompson would be to see it again.

He looked in the stores, and the barber shop, and the bank. Then he saw Mr. Thompson's team standing on a side street, in front of Mr. Paddock's wagon-shop. He opened the door of the long, low building, and went in.

Mr. Paddock and Mr. Thompson were standing by the round-bellied stove, looking at a piece of hickory and talking about it. Almanzo waited, because he could not interrupt them.

It was warm in the building, and there was a good smell of shavings and leather and paint. Beyond the stove two workmen were making a wagon, and another was painting thin red lines on the red spokes of a new buggy. The buggy glistened proudly in black paint. Long curls of shavings lay in heaps, and the whole place was as pleasant as a barn on a rainy day. The workmen whistled while they measured and marked and sawed and planed the clean-smelling wood.

353

Mr. Thompson was arguing about the price of a new wagon. Almanzo decided that Mr. Paddock did not like Mr. Thompson, but he was trying to sell the wagon. He figured the cost with his big carpenter's pencil, and soothingly tried to persuade Mr. Thompson.

"You see, I can't cut the price any further and pay my men," he said. "I'm doing the best I can for you. I guarantee we'll make a wagon to please you, or you don't have to take it."

"Well, maybe I'll come back to you, if I can't do better elsewhere," Mr. Thompson said, suspiciously.

"Glad to serve you any time," said Mr. Paddock. Then he saw Almanzo, and asked him how the pig was getting along. Almanzo liked big, jolly Mr. Paddock; he always asked about Lucy.

"She'll weigh around a hundred and fifty now," Almanzo told him, then he turned to Mr. Thompson and asked, "Did you lose a pocketbook?"

354

Mr. Thompson jumped. He clapped a hand to his pocket, and fairly shouted.

"Yes, I have! Fifteen hundred dollars in it, too. What about it? What do you know about it?"

"Is this it?" Almanzo asked.

"Yes, yes, yes, that's it!" Mr. Thompson said, snatching the pocketbook. He opened it and hurriedly counted the money. He counted all the bills over twice, and he looked exactly like a man skinning a flea for its hide and tallow.

Then he breathed a long sigh of relief, and said, "Well, this durn boy didn't steal any of it."

Almanzo's face was hot as fire. He wanted to hit Mr. Thompson.

Mr. Thompson thrust his skinny hand into his pants pocket and hunted around. He took out something.

"Here," he said, putting in into Almanzo's hand. It was a nickel.

Almanzo was so angry he couldn't see. He hated Mr. Thompson; he wanted to hurt him.

355

Mr. Thompson called him a durn boy, and as good as called him a thief. Almanzo didn't want his old nickel. Suddenly he thought what to say.

"Here," he said, handing the nickel back. "Keep your nickel. I can't change it."

Mr. Thompson's tight, mean face turned red. One of the workmen laughed a short, jeering laugh. But Mr. Paddock stepped up to Mr. Thompson, angry.

"Don't you call this boy a thief, Thompson!" he said. "And he's not a beggar, either! That's how you treat him, is it? When he brings you back your fifteen hundred dollars! Call him a thief and hand him a nickel, will you?"

Mr. Thompson stepped back, but Mr. Paddock stepped right after him. Mr. Paddock shook his fist under Mr. Thompson's nose.

"You measly skinflint!" Mr. Paddock said. "Not if I know it, you won't! Not in my place! A good, honest, decent little chap, and you— For a cent I'll— No! You hand him a hundred of that money, and do it quick! No, two hundred! Two hundred dollars, I say, or take the consequences!"

Mr. Thompson tried to say something, and
so did Almanzo. But Mr. Paddock's fists

clenched and the muscles of his arms bulged. "Two hundred!" he shouted. "Hand it over, quick! Or I'll see you do!"

Mr. Thompson shrank down small, watching Mr. Paddock, and he licked his thumb and hurriedly counted off some bills. He held them out to Almanzo. Almanzo said, "Mr. Paddock—"

"Now get out of here, if you know what's healthy! Get out!" Mr. Paddock said, and before Almanzo could blink he was standing there with the bills in his hand, and Mr. Thompson slammed the door behind himself.

Almanzo was so excited he stammered. He said he didn't think Father would like it. Almanzo felt queer about taking all that money, and yet he did want to keep it. Mr. Paddock said he would talk to Father; he rolled down his shirt sleeves and put on his coat and asked:

"Where is he?"

Almanzo almost ran, to keep up with Mr. Paddock's long strides. The bills were clutched tight in his hand. Father was putting packages

358

into the wagon, and Mr. Paddock told him what had happened.

"For a cent I'd have smashed his sneering face," Mr. Paddock said. "But it struck me that giving up cash is what hurts him most. And I figure the boy's entitled to it."

"I don't know as anyone's entitled to anything for common honesty," Father objected. "Though I must say I appreciate the spirit you showed, Paddock."

"I don't say he deserved more than decent gratitude for giving Thompson his own money," Mr. Paddock said. "But it's too much to ask him to stand and take insults, on top of that. I say Almanzo's entitled to that two hundred."

"Well, there's something in what you say," said Father. Finally he decided, "All right, son, you can keep that money."

Almanzo smoothed out the bills and looked at them; two hundred dollars. That was as much as the horse-buyer paid for one of Father's four-year-olds.

359

"And I'm much obliged to you, Paddock, standing up for the boy the way you did," Father said.

"Well, I can afford to lose a customer now and then, in a good cause," said Mr. Paddock. He asked Almanzo, "What are you going to do with all that money?"

Almanzo looked at Father. "Could I put it in the bank?" he asked.

"That's the place to put money," said Father. "Well, well, well, two hundred dollars! I was twice your age before I had so much."

"So was I. Yes, and older than that," Mr. Paddock said.

Father and Almanzo went to the bank. Almanzo could just look over the ledge at the cashier sitting on his high stool with a pen behind his ear. The cashier craned to look down at Almanzo and asked Father: "Hadn't I better put this down to your account, sir?"

"No," said Father. "It's the boy's money; let him handle it himself. He won't learn any younger."

360

"Yes, sir," the cashier said. Almanzo had to write his name twice. Then the cashier carefully counted the bills, and wrote Almanzo's name in a little book. He wrote the figures, $200, in the book, and he gave the book to Almanzo.

Almanzo went out of the bank with Father, and asked him:

"How do I get the money out again?"

"You ask for it, and they'll give it to you. But remember this, son; as long as that money's in the bank, it's working for you. Every dollar in the bank is making you four cents a year. That's a sight easier than you can earn money any other way. Any time you want to spend a nickel, you stop and think how much work it takes to earn a dollar."

"Yes, Father," Almanzo said. He was thinking that he had more than enough money to buy a little colt. He could break a little colt of his own; he could teach it everything. Father would never let him break one of his colts.

But this was not the end of that exciting day.

Chapter 29.

Farmer Boy

MR. PADDOCK met Almanzo and Father outside the bank. He told Father that he had something in mind.

"I've been meaning to speak about it for some little time," he said. "About this boy of yours."

Almanzo was surprised.

"You ever think of making a wheelwright out of him?" Mr. Paddock asked.

"Well, no," Father answered slowly, "I can't say as I ever did."

"Well, think it over now," said Mr. Paddock. "It's a growing business, Wilder. The country's growing, population getting bigger all the time, and folks have got to have wagons and buggies. They've got to travel back and forth. The railroads don't hurt us. We're getting more customers all the time. It's a good opening for a smart young fellow."

"Yes," Father said.

"I've got no sons of my own, and you've got two," said Mr. Paddock. "You'll have to think about starting Almanzo out in life, before long. Apprentice him to me, and I'll treat the boy right. If he turns out the way I expect, no reason he shouldn't have the business, in time. He'd be a rich man, with maybe half a hundred workmen under him. It's worth thinking about."

"Yes," Father said. "Yes, it's worth thinking about. I appreciate what you've said, Paddock."

Father did not talk on the way home. Almanzo sat beside him on the wagon seat and did not say anything, either. So much had happened that he thought about it all together, all mixed up.

He thought of the cashier's inky fingers, and of Mr. Thompson's thin mouth screwed down at the corners, and of Mr. Paddock's fists, and the busy, warm, cheerful wagon-shop. He thought, if he was Mr. Paddock's apprentice, he wouldn't have to go to school.

He had often envied Mr. Paddock's workmen. Their work was fascinating. The thin, long shavings curled away from the keen edges of the planes. They stroked the smooth wood with their fingers. Almanzo liked to do that, too. He would like to spread on paint with the wide paint-brush, and he would like to make fine, straight lines with the tiny pointed brush.

When a buggy was done, all shining in its new paint, or when a wagon was finished, every piece good sound hickory or oak, with the wheels painted red and the box painted green, and a little picture painted on the tailboard, the workmen were proud. They made wagons as sturdy as Father's bobsleds, and far more beautiful.

Then Almanzo felt the small, stiff bankbook

in his pocket, and he thought about a colt. He wanted a colt with slender legs and large, gentle, wondering eyes, like Starlight's. He wanted to teach the little colt everything, as he had taught Star and Bright.

So Father and Almanzo rode all the way home, not saying anything. The air was still and cold and all the trees were like black lines drawn on the snow and the sky.

It was chore-time when they got home. Almanzo helped do the chores, but he wasted some time looking at Starlight. He stroked the soft velvety nose, and he ran his hand along the firm curve of Starlight's little neck, under the mane. Starlight nibbled with soft lips along his sleeve.

"Son, where be you?" Father called, and Almanzo ran guiltily to his milking.

At supper-time he sat steadily eating, while Mother talked about what had happened. She said that never in her life—! She said you could have knocked her over with a feather, and she didn't know why it was so hard to get it all out of Father. Father answered her questions, but

365

like Almanzo, he was busy eating. At last Mother asked him:

"James, what's on your mind?"

Then Father told her that Mr. Paddock wanted to take Almanzo as an apprentice.

Mother's brown eyes snapped, and her cheeks turned as red as her red wool dress. She laid down her knife and fork.

"I never heard of such a thing!" she said. "Well, the sooner Mr. Paddock gets that out of his head, the better! I hope you gave him a piece of your mind! Why on earth, I'd like to know, should Almanzo live in town at the beck and call of every Tom, Dick, and Harry!"

"Paddock makes good money," said Father. "I guess if truth were told, he banks more money every year than I do. He looks on it as a good opening for the boy."

"Well!" Mother snapped. She was all ruffled, like an angry hen. "A pretty pass the world's coming to, if any man thinks it's a step up in the world to leave a good farm and go to town! How does Mr. Paddock make his money, if it isn't catering to us? I guess if he didn't make wagons to suit farmers, he wouldn't last long!"

"That's true enough," said Father. "But——"

"There's no 'but' about it!" Mother said. "Oh, it's bad enough to see Royal come down to being nothing but a storekeeper! Maybe he'll make money, but he'll never be the man you are. Truckling to other people for his living, all his days— He'll never be able to call his soul his own."

For a minute Almanzo wondered if Mother was going to cry.

"There, there," Father said, sadly. "Don't take it too much to heart. Maybe it's all for the best, somehow."

"I won't have Almanzo going the same way!" Mother cried. "I won't have it, you hear me?"

"I feel the same way you do," said Father. "But the boy'll have to decide. We can keep him here on the farm by law till he's twenty-one, but it won't do any good if he's wanting

to go. No. If Almanzo feels the way Royal does, we better apprentice him to Paddock while he's young enough."

Almanzo went on eating. He was listening, but he was tasting the good taste of roast pork and apple sauce in every corner of his mouth. He took a long, cold drink of milk, and then he sighed and tucked his napkin farther in, and he reached for his pumpkin pie.

He cut off the quivering point of golden-brown pumpkin, dark with spices and sugar. It melted on his tongue, and all his mouth and nose were spicy.

"He's too young to know his own mind," Mother objected.

Almanzo took another big mouthful of pie. He could not speak till he was spoken to, but he thought to himself that he was old enough to know he'd rather be like Father than like anybody else. He did not want to be like Mr. Paddock, even. Mr. Paddock had to please a mean man like Mr. Thompson, or lose the sale of a wagon. Father was free and independent; if he went out of his way to please anybody, it was because he wanted to.

Suddenly he realized that Father had spoken to him. He swallowed, and almost choked on pie. "Yes, Father," he said.

Father was looking solemn. "Son," he said, "you heard what Paddock said about you being apprenticed to him?"

"Yes, Father."

"What do you say about it?"

Almanzo didn't exactly know what to say. He hadn't supposed he could say anything. He would have to do whatever Father said.

"Well, son, you think about it," said Father. "I want you should make up your own mind. With Paddock, you'd have an easy life, in some ways. You wouldn't be out in all kinds of weather. Cold winter nights, you could lie snug in bed and not worry about young stock freezing. Rain or shine, wind or snow, you'd be under shelter. You'd be shut up, inside walls. Likely you'd always have plenty to eat and wear and money in the bank."

"James!" Mother said.

"That's the truth, and we must be fair about it," Father answered. "But there's the other side, too, Almanzo. You'd have to depend on other folks, son, in town. Everything you got, you'd get from other folks.

"A farmer depends on himself, and the land and the weather. If you're a farmer, you raise what you eat, you raise what you wear, and you keep warm with wood out of your own

370

timber. You work hard, but you work as you please, and no man can tell you to go or come. You'll be free and independent, son, on a farm."

Almanzo squirmed. Father was looking at him too hard, and so was Mother. Almanzo did not want to live inside walls and please people he didn't like, and never have horses and cows and fields. He wanted to be just like Father. But he didn't want to say so.

"You take your time, son. Think it over," Father said. "You make up your mind what you want."

"Father!" Almanzo exclaimed.

"Yes, son?"

"Can I? Can I really tell you what I want?"

"Yes, son," Father encouraged him.

"I want a colt," Almanzo said. "Could I buy a colt all my own with some of that two hundred dollars, and would you let me break him?"

Father's beard slowly widened with a smile. He put down his napkin and leaned back in his chair and looked at Mother. Then he turned to Almanzo and said:

"Son, you leave that money in the bank."

Almanzo felt everything sinking down inside him. And then, suddenly, the whole world was a great, shining, expanding glow of warm light. For Father went on:

"If it's a colt you want, I'll give you Starlight."

"Father!" Almanzo gasped. "For my very own?"

"Yes, son. You can break him, and drive him, and when he's a four-year-old you can sell him or keep him, just as you want to. We'll take him out on a rope, first thing tomorrow morning, and you can begin to gentle him."